PlanningTo Die

A Matthew Diggerson Mystery

by

D.G.Gillespie

For information, email **Cozy Cat Press**, cozycatpress@aol.com or visit our website at: www.cozycatpress.com

COZY CAT
P R E S S

ISBN: 978-1-946063-38-0

Printed in the United States of America

Cover design by Paula Ellenberger
www.paulaellenberger.com

1 2 3 4 5 6 7 8 9 10

Dedicated to my mother and father (Ruth and Robert), both of whom fostered two great forces in my life: books and nature.

Table of Contents

Chapter One: Organizational Strategies

To build strong supporting paragraphs, you need to organize their content, to use a plan for each, so this simple definition will help: Add a topic sentence (TS) and STIR at least twice. Standing for STructural points, Illustrations, and Reasoning, STIR reminds you to break down the TS into narrowed supporting points, to illustrate each point so that you show rather than just tell, and to provide reasoning that links the "I" to the "ST," not assuming that the reader can see the connection. When you plan, you think, helping both yourself and the reader.

Digger felt fine. First off, the early-October day offered just the type of sky Matthew Diggerson liked most: mostly cloudy. The night before had brought rain, which dragged with it the day's armada of white, empty cumulous blobs, rimmed in molten gold by the sun. *A religious looking sky*, Digger would call it although he himself believed in no higher deity. Digger needed just Anna—his wife for a handful of fairly easy years, his soul connection—and his work, both spouse and vocation providing the writing teacher with a sense of self, of fitting well into existence. In fact, this semester was Digger's first with a change of schedule, the typical 8 a.m. classes transitioning into what he really wanted, a later start to the day, in his case 11 a.m. as his earliest class. Prior to this fall semester, for all nine years of his college career—the first two at Sea View Community College, the next seven at Ocean View College (five as an adjunct, the last two as a full-time faculty member in the Humanities Department)—Digger had been assigned an early-morning schedule. Eight o'clock classes, forced on adjuncts (part-timers) and freshmen, were often disparaged, even by Digger. A year earlier, approaching the room of his 8 a.m. college composition class, the young professor had seen just a dark hole and had thought, *Where is everyone?* Upon flicking up the room's light switch, he had found his students all sitting silently in their five rows of chairs, all looking forward at him. The strange scene had startled Digger, making him laugh, more of an exclamation than mirth, though. In that moment, he had realized that the image of those motionless students, slumbering yet stiff, would stay with him forever.

That year-old class had been a turning point of sorts in Matthew Diggerson's somewhat young teaching career because for half of that spring semester he just could not get the students to talk. He had asked questions about models, enquired about their positions on various topics, requested their views on readings, called for volunteers to put sentences on the board, and stood in frustrated silence as they all sat mute. Digger had been perplexed because when he talked to the students individually, they were all friendly and apparently sociable. In a big group, though, they transformed into zombies.

He had told Anna about the quiet class many times, so once a week she had asked about the zombies. One night at dinner, she had said, "Matt [most people called him 'Digger,' but not Anna or his mother], what do those zombies want most?"

"I guess," Digger had replied, "to not be in my class," and then he had chuckled.

"Exactly," Anna had said, laughing, too, "but it has nothing to do with your class, it's with all classes. They just don't want to be in class. So if they participate, you should give them a chance to leave early."

"Like a get-out-of-jail-for-free card?" Digger had said.

And then Anna had given him a great idea: "Freedom chips! Bring some poker chips to class and toss them out to people who participate."

Freedom Chips? Warming to the idea immediately, loving the label, too, Digger had said, "Maybe different colors could mean different times—one minute, two." Digger knew that Anna had been onto something, and now that his mind had been twisted a bit, he had seen the possibilities and put them into action. During the next 8 a.m. class that semester, Digger had carried a couple dozen red, blue, and white poker chips to class, announcing them as "Freedom Chips" and explaining what they meant: one free minute for each honest, thoughtful student response (no matter the chip's color). Within twenty minutes of that class, Digger had tossed out all the chips, but a strange thing happened: the students kept talking, even without the reward of an early exit. The flood of participation had begun.

He had used the poker chips in all his classes, which all became more lively and enthusiastic, so he went further, creating a variety of lesson plans that offered students a chance to win their way out early, to earn minutes. *Learn and earn!* This fall semester, he had experimented with such lessons, which had transformed his classes (from passive to active) and infused him with even more spirit than usual. In fact, while the fall semester's longest month, October, often ground at students and teachers alike—no end in sight, no finish to the work and the responsibilities—Digger still felt fresh. Entering his third year as a full-timer, Professor Diggerson still basked in the security of his life—happily married, successfully employed, his track ahead as straight and sure as the Ocean View sidewalk that led from faculty parking to his office in the Faculty Office Building, a long walk but pleasant, buoyed by many buildings against the winds that always seemed to blow from the sea, and especially enjoyable on October days such as this, with blue skies peeking out behind cotton clouds, not too warm, not too cool, just right. Then he saw the worm.

Pushed by the overnight rains onto the concrete, the earthworm was moving its raised head (Digger supposed it was the head, anyway) back and forth, swaying like a snake, its tail like a little pendulum, too, and the teacher's mind went back in time, back some seven years, to the first time he took this walk. A little more than seven years ago, it had been a wet morning in July, a little steamy even, and as he stepped from the parking lot onto the sidewalk's beginning, he had looked down to see a fat gray earthworm nosing its way blindly across the concrete. It had looked a little pathetic, determined but doomed. Thinking that the worm would be stepped on sooner or later, Digger had bent down, scooped it up with his right hand fingers, and tossed the gray string into the safety of the grass. His fingers had felt mainly wet, just a little sticky. Feeling satisfied, he had continued his walk—which would end at a place called the Faculty Offices Building, Room 311, where he would interview for a part-time composition teaching position for the fall semester—and soon spotted another earthworm, this one firmly stuck to the sidewalk's middle, miles away from a good life. He scooped and tossed it, too, and then the worm two steps after it, and the one after that. At that point, Digger had looked up the sidewalk, stretched straight to the sea, or so it seemed, and had seen dozens of worms, maybe even hundreds. *What the hell!* he had thought. *I'll be late for my meeting!* As he stepped and scooped, bent and stood, Digger had cleared a couple dozen of the earthworms from the sidewalk, and his right-hand fingers felt a little disgusting. Imagining an important person with her arm out in greeting (he was supposed to meet with a Professor Gwena Schmidt), Digger had sought a rest room in the Faculty Offices Building before venturing up the stairs to the third floor and his successful meeting. He had been hired that day, had served as an adjunct faculty member for five years, and then been elevated to full-time status.

On this October day, two years after his elevation, the gray groping earthworm was basically by himself (or herself—couldn't earthworms be both at the same time?), so Digger bent down, flipped his hand over to see the creature, said "Hello, little fellow," and underhanded the small, simple life form into the grass. Before reaching the first building, housing the school's president, the administrators, and Tutorial Services, where Digger had tutored for the past seven years, the writing teacher had "saved" just three more worms, a far cry from seven years ago.

The Admin Building sported a folksy first-floor open-air porch that wrapped around the front and one side of the building, OVC's only wooden structure, only two stories high, too, unlike the school's other four-storied monoliths of modern brick. The Admin Building always seemed out of place to Digger, as though the rest of OVC had been built around it some fifty years ago. Seeing the sign for Tutorial Services, in the basement of the Admin Building, Digger felt fine again about his decision to no longer tutor for Don Domberg, the head of TS and a fellow full-time composition instructor. Digger pictured Professor Domberg down those stairs, probably seated in his office, calling out the door to someone and laughing.

White teeth flashing within his great beard. With the years, Don's thick facial hair had expanded, and Digger wondered why anyone would cultivate such a thing below their nose. Don didn't seem particularly religious. Maybe it was a control thing, maybe even a mask. The beard shovel inflated the man's head by about 30 percent, and maybe that was the answer: Don wanted a big head. Why do people do anything? *Because they want to. Just like me,* thought Digger, who now spent only six or so hours per day at OVC, not the eight or more on past tutoring days, so that he could devote more time to Anna.

She had been going through something, Digger had finally admitted to himself. Had to be her job, which could be a little depressing. Anna told him stories about the special-education children, about her school's policies in stopping certain behaviors, such as flicking, which was what it sounded like: The boy or girl would stand or sit in a daze, just opening and closing their hands quickly, repeatedly. The staff didn't care for flicking, and Anna had been taught to stop it. Digger had forgotten how, something Anna called "primitive." He would have to ask her again. She told him nice stories, too, such as the one about Tommy, her main "student," a young autistic boy who loved trees. When they went outside, Tommy would yell "Treeeeeeeeee!" and run to one, throwing his arms around it. Of course, the staff would have trouble yanking Tommy off the tree. Anna would have just left him there, and Digger remembered saying to her, "Yeah, I wish everyone loved trees that much."

Work issues. Digger could understand those. Anna couldn't be troubled about the cottage; it had been exactly what they had wanted: a connection with nature and disconnection with humanity. They had both wanted a private place to live, and for two years now they had enjoyed their new home, which came with a stretch of beach even though the cottage faced the bay, not the open Atlantic. The air was still full of salt and wind and gulls, and only in the summer did they ever look out their back windows and see anyone.

What was wrong with Anna? Digger asked himself that question occasionally, but he didn't ask her. He was busy with the still-new seeming fall semester, with all the responsibilities of a full-timer—the students he had to advise, the meetings he had to attend, the committees he was steered to join, the scholarly papers he was asked to review (and sometimes write), not to mention the four classes to teach and all the papers to critique and sometimes grade. *Life was full.* They had talked once about getting a dog—maybe that's what Anna needed. She had never wanted kids, a fact that made Digger laugh considering her choice of career. But maybe that was partly why she didn't want them: She saw what could happen and felt the burdens.

Now that Digger realized it, Anna had not gone with him on a beach walk all semester (more than five weeks), and they even watched TV together less. Just this past Friday, Anna had come home far later than usual, close to 9 o'clock, and then just gone to bed with hardly a hello or any explanation, just an "out with friends" as she passed through the small living room. *What friends?* Within the five years of marriage, Digger's pool of old college pals and even a couple of high school ones had dried up because he spent all of his free time with her. He wanted to, chose to. Anna had filled his life, and his old friends had moved away or had kids, drifting off either physically or mentally. Since a couple with a child or two didn't mix well with one without, Anna and Digger had slowly separated from past social alliances. Digger didn't need anyone but Anna, anyway.

Walking, he was glad not to see any more worms, but just past the Administration Building, Digger noticed an approaching student, remembered him at once: *Danny Something?* He had tutored him last semester in the basement of the building just passed. The boy had seemed slightly autistic. Digger remembered that Danny Something was not a strong writer and not very sociable or happy. Compared to this student, Anna these days was the life of the party.

The sidewalk where Digger and Danny Something would soon cross paths ran across the north-side of Ocean View College's campus, so it wasn't as busy as the center walkway, which Digger could see was crowded with groups of students heading to class, to the library, or maybe to an early lunch. Alone, head down, the approaching student stood out for two other reasons: One, he was black, and because OVC was a private school, minorities often could not afford the tuition; two, as mentioned, Digger recognized his former tutee from last spring, Digger's final semester at Tutorial Services.

A few steps away from the solitary, somewhat short figure, Digger greeted him, startling the young man, who Digger realized must be a sophomore but had yet to take the sudden physical spurt that turned a freshman into an adult.

"Oh!" said Danny, and Digger remembered his last name: *Jones.*

"You seem to be deep in thought, Danny."

The boy did in fact seem to be thinking, but then he looked into Digger's eyes: "Professor Diggerson, hello." A smile flickered but went out.

"Are you worried about a class, about a writing assignment? Can I help you?" Digger kept his eyes on Danny Jones, but the latter gazed more at the ground than at Digger, who wondered (as he had before) if Danny weren't just a bit off mentally, maybe autistic.

"No, not really," said Danny, adding "I don't have much writing to do this semester. Except in my writing class. I have to retake the one I failed last semester."

"I'm sorry to hear that," said Digger, and he was sorry. Although tutoring the boy had shown Digger that Danny needed a lot of help with his writing, he had not realized that Danny had failed the class outright.

"Do you know why you failed? I don't remember your teacher? Was it Professor Schmidt?"

"I never turned in my last paper," said the boy, looking up and then down. Digger waited, thinking that he could use a freedom chip or two, but then Danny spoke again. "I did have Professor Schmidt. Some people called her the Grammar Nazi. She was tough. I'm a bad writer."

Digger had long ago heard about that somewhat shocking nickname, but since most people used it as a dark joke (both students and colleagues), the name Grammar Nazi no longer surprised Digger. "Professor Schmidt knows her grammar, but she's a really nice person. Do you have her again?"

"No," said Danny Jones, and then he added, "Professor Smith."

Paul Smith, thought Digger, *now there's a grammar Nazi*. Danny Jones had not caught any breaks. Keeping that thought to himself, Digger said, "You'll get better. Writing just takes little pieces of knowledge and then skills, and once you know more and practice those skills, you will become much stronger. It takes time, Danny."

"Yeah," said Danny, and he looked again at the sidewalk. Digger thought of worms. He realized, too, that the boy wanted to resume his trek.

"Listen, Danny, if you want some help, I'm no longer at Tutorial Services, but I'm in the Faculty Offices Building every afternoon, especially on Tuesdays and Thursdays. So feel free to come see me. I'd really like to help. Knowledge and practice, that's what it takes."

"Thanks, Professor Diggerson," said Danny Jones, disengaging, head lowering, moving off like a little life boat from a sinking ship. In this case, the smaller vessel seemed more in peril.

Watching the sad fellow shuffle off, Digger didn't want to sever the connection, so he called to the boy: "Danny, watch out for the worms!"

The student half raised his left arm but didn't turn. He did seem to be watching out for worms. Digger wondered why he would yell such an absurd thing since nobody else seemed to care about the earthworms. Colleagues made fun of Digger about it: One once even called him Worm Man, as though Digger were a neurotic super hero. What was his super power? Advanced empathy? The ability to create symbolism? Watch out for the worms: nobody could dispute that advice.

After one last look at Danny, Digger turned and continued his long walk to the Faculty Offices Building. Before passing by the next building, housing mainly social sciences classes, Digger noticed a knot of youth approaching, *a goggle of Goths*, he labeled them due to their dark clothes and pale faces. Most OVC students looked well-kept, for lack of a better adjective, in other words content and rich, and Digger imagined that many would graduate into the family businesses that paid for their four-year tuition. But this Goth pack wouldn't, not without makeovers and a wardrobe change. The group of five or six (hard to tell) darkly dressed youths looked out of place on this campus, like crows in a blossoming cherry tree, and Digger had noticed them first last year. One of the Goths was even one of his current students (Digger wanted to call him John or James—some "J" name, anyway), but the J-ster didn't appear ready to greet his composition mentor. The five students, Digger now saw, just cackled amongst themselves, and Digger had to admit that their little shrieks and guffaws made him feel a bit old, a bit lonely. The three boys and two girls all quieted up when reaching Digger, who said "hello" but received no reply, just a nod from John or Jacob (Josh?), who had studs—spikes?—on his shoulders, making Digger think of Oakland Raider football fans. The crows started hooting again a few paces into Digger's passing, but he, like Danny Jones, did not turn back.

He should have told the Goths to watch out for the worms, Digger thought sarcastically, pondering and disliking the power of groups. Then he thought that maybe the worms should watch out for the pale humans, who looked like they could use some protein. *Worms, the grave, death.* Funny how a mood could change so quickly. Maybe he should check into the social sciences building and have his brain analyzed. After that thought, Digger spotted another worm, this one a little pink and hardly moving, so he bent and lifted the limp little life form off the concrete, leaving it in the manicured dirt at the end of Social Sciences. He didn't think that the small creature had much of a future.

Dropping that thought, Digger glanced to the left at the library, another brick upon brick edifice, a declaration of purpose and permanence, this one sporting two tower extensions, one on either end of the building, which from the front looked a little like a fat, squat "H" with the lower half filled in. Someone had once told Digger that the towers represented lighthouses, but since neither one narrowed to a lighted top, Digger had never gotten that mariner's sense of possibilities from the architecture. Instead of lights, both towers offered time in the form of big square clocks, and Digger noticed that it was now 10:37 or 10:38. The two clocks never agreed. *Just like people*, Digger thought. Either way, he was early. His eyes on the unembellished towers, Digger decided once again that what Ocean View College needed was a scattering of looming rooftop gargoyles, especially atop the library's towers, to give the campus more depth. But maybe the gulls did that, dipping and soaring and calling out to each other and to time, or maybe the towering Bay Bridge, that connected the towns of Ocean View and Bayside, the two sides of the bay, and housed the gargoyles on its peaks, its two great shoulders, too high in the sky to reveal crouching monsters. Glancing up and forward, Digger could see the great bridge rising above the nearby trees and tearing across the sky, its dark-green paint showing clearly beneath the sun.

Digger looked earthward again as he walked. *No worms here*. Due to October's hint of winter, only a few earthworms had followed the night rain onto the sidewalk, just the big hearty ones mainly, and then Digger's mind slipped back to the fragile and doomed little pink worm. The others must have nosed their tube faces against the concrete, received some primitive message of flight, and returned to the moist, grainy soil.

Before reaching OVC's next brick-faced building, another attractive but fairly non-descript structure, the Business School, Digger saw another little group of students approaching, noticing another of his current students, Amanda, who liked to be called Mandy. She walked smiling between two males—one who would look at place hoisting a sail, the other appearing somewhat comical (*a big neck*, thought Digger)—and all three students locked eyes with the composition teacher.

"Hello, Mandy," said Digger pleasantly, and she and the sailor smiled back and greeted him (Big Neck looked a little confused). *That was nice,* thought Digger, and then he heard the trio laughing and wondered whether no gulf was so large—not race, religion, gender, economic class—as age, the gap between youth and everyone else. Digger was only 33 (*Christ's age,* he thought), but he remembered being 21 and thinking that anyone over 24 was ancient. *This place would be more enjoyable if there were no students*, Digger summarized sarcastically.

As Digger neared his destination at last, the campus sloped down to the sea, the Bay Bridge expanding just beyond it. The Faculty Offices Building was the furthest southern structure (except for the older dormitories), the closest to the open Atlantic, the head of the sleeping giant, so to speak, which lay along the bay's mouth. Ocean View College exuded sea and space, many of the trees on this end being somewhat squatted, as ocean-rimmed trees tended to be due to their branches fighting constant wind and their roots searching despairingly through sandy soil. Toward the wide water loomed OVC's main landmark, the Bay Bridge, curving from Ocean View Drive and rising into the suspension bridge's two gothic towers (*gargoyles?*) and then descending somewhat sharply down to Bayside on the far shore. Down here, close up, the bridge looked like a see-through mountain, a heavy sketch in the sky, thick lines. Some called it the Bye-Bye Bridge since for decades beaten down humans had climbed up its narrow walkways to touch the clouds and find solace in the cold depths below.

Out of the FOB's center doorway, Digger suddenly saw Gwena Schmidt stride forth: the Grammar Nazi herself! Gwena had been one of the two people—along with Dean Kozar—who had hired Digger seven years ago, and she had been Humanities (i.e., Writing) Department Chair all those years. At the interview, the dean had asked Digger about his impression of the school, and Digger had said, "It's a beautiful campus, has a very open feeling, a lot of sky." And then he had added, "has a lot of earthworms." Dean Kozar and Professor Schmidt had laughed loudly at that, and Digger had known suddenly that the job was his.

Gwena had taught at OVC for thirty-five years, one of the towers at the school, as prominent in a way as the Bay Bridge's peaked shoulders. Thin, tall (as tall as Digger, though that wasn't saying a whole lot for her physical ascension), cheekbones that jutted like apples, eyes like lasers (blue and deep), Professor Schmidt fit in perfectly with the medieval bridge looming behind her, both looking timeless and formidable. Digger had met her husband over a year ago, and Richard Schmidt looked much like his wife, the King and Queen of the chessboard. When Digger saw Gwena, he always imagined her cropped with a cylindrical mantle that reached even higher to the sky, connecting her even more solidly to the gods. Gwena had a presence (perhaps an aura) that both welcomed and warned— nice to see you and don't say anything stupid!

"Digger!" she greeted him, showing two rows of perfect teeth.

"Hi, Gwena," said Digger.

"I just told Paul Smith a joke that one of Richard's stock broker buddies told him."

"Let's hear it," said Digger, expecting a bit of ribaldry.

"What are the three most dangerous wrestling holds?" Gwena's eyes and cheeks and teeth all shone, and Digger thought of a bronze statue and then of wrestling.

"Wrestling holds?" he said to buy some time.

Gwena didn't often suffer time. "One, the Full Nelson [Digger recognized the term]. Two, the Half Nelson [*Of course*, thought Digger—*Full and Half, but what?*]. Three, the Father Nelson [*What! Oh, hoh!*]."

Digger laughed honestly, both professors ho-hoing into the cooling October air.

"I'm going to tell that joke to Anna, but don't repeat it to Human Resources," laughed Digger. "It's against their diversity training, making fun of a minority, pedophile priests."

"Oh, to Hell with HR," said Gwena, making Digger laugh again (more inside this time). "I'm retiring after this year anyway. They can't catch me if I'm not on campus. Yes, tell that joke to Anna."

Digger had known that this year would be Gwena's final one at OVC, and he didn't like that fact at all. He didn't like change. He said, "You're too young to retire, Gwena. Don't go. The place won't be the same without you."

"Without the Grammar Nazi, you mean," she laughed, making fun of the nickname created by long-ago students to make good-natured fun of her. As a faculty tutor, Digger had seen most of his peers' directions sheets, and hers had highlighted a long list of bulleted Do's and Don't's, one of the latter being "Do not use 'is.'" She had bolded the "not" and the "is," too, and another Don't was "Do not begin a sentence with 'because,'" advice that Digger had heard other students repeat, a common tip that made no sense to Digger unless past teachers were trying to get students to avoid fragments. "Because" was Digger's favorite word, and he advised students to use it often and everywhere (and to substitute "since" at times to avoid repetitive diction). After seeing Gwena's bulleted list, he had laughed at the "is" point and told the young fellow that he definitely agreed with his professor due to weak verbs creating wordiness, whereupon Gwena's student had declared, "The Grammar Nazi takes off points if we use 'is'!" Digger had then explained why "is" often caused wordiness, thinking that Gwena probably had just *said* that she would take off points. He had never asked her about that, though.

"When I first heard a student use that nickname," Digger said to the Humanities Chair, "the guy said it in such a nice way that I laughed."

"Nazis are not often funny subjects."

"No, but I always liked the way students said it. I wonder how many of them even know who the Nazis were."

"Before their parents' time even, and that great generation is dying off, something like one hundred every day."

Digger had heard a similar fact, but in his head he remembered a thousand per day. Gwena was probably right. "You're like Hogan's Heroes," said Digger. "A nice Nazi."

"Thank you, Digger. The nickname fits, so I wear it. Richard thinks it's rude, but grammar is important, not taught enough anymore. If I embody it, then so much the better."

Digger actually thought that grammar was taught too much, that having students do handbook exercises—for run-ons, fragments, comma use, etc.—didn't really work, because the editing skills failed to transfer to students' own processes. He did, though, agree that clean, concise prose communicated best. "I love that you don't allow 'is,'" he said in response.

"Oh, I tell them that, Digger, and occasionally I take a point or two off just to provide some bite with the bark. They need to see consequences."

Digger agreed and then switched subjects a bit, the words "bite" and "consequences" making him think of sad Danny Jones, the lonely black boy with his head down.

"I just saw a student of yours, Gwena, from last spring. Do you remember Danny Jones? I tutored him a couple times last semester."

"Danny Jones? Was he the African-American boy, the one who never said a word? I had to fail him. He never submitted his last essay. Had he done so, he would probably have just scraped by, but we can't save all these students. We can just give them advice and hope that they take it. Who has Danny now?"

"Paul Smith."

"Speak of the devil," laughed the older woman, no doubt because she had just mentioned telling Paul the wrestling joke. "From the Grammar Nazi to the Ancient Grammarian—if Danny Jones survives, he will be all the stronger for it!"

"That's true," Digger laughed, and then his eyes were drawn past his favorite colleague, past the squat and sturdy Faculty Offices Building (four brick stories but lowered by the sloping lawn to the sea), past even a pair of soaring, slicing gulls, to the Bay Bridge itself, one peak gleaming greenly within a fat sun ray, the further shoulder shadowed by cloud, dark. *The two faces of life.*

"Have to get going," said Gwena Schmidt, but then she asked Digger a question: "Been picking up worms, have you?"

Digger smiled. "It's one of those days. Watch out for the worms."

"Hm," said the Chair. "Symbolic advice."

Then the FOB door opened abruptly and spit Tobias Mann, another full-time composition instructor, out into the sun and shade. The office grapevine said that Mann wanted Gwena's job, but the gaunt professor had said nothing about that desire to Digger and today just passed wordlessly by both peers, giving them (or maybe just Gwena) a quick nod.

"Is Tobias growing a little beard?" asked Digger, who thought he had seen a thin triangle below his colleague's mouth.

"Makes him look even more like the devil," said Professor Schmidt. Then she walked off the path behind Mann, saying, "Watch out for the worms, Digger."

That was good advice, *whether the worms be friend or foe.*

Chapter Two: Introductions

Planning is needed for all essay paragraphs, not just for supporting ones. To start a college composition, think the 3 T's: Tease, Topic, and Thesis. To begin, offer a Tease, a hook to capture the reader's interest, perhaps an interesting quotation, a startling statistic, the beginning of a brief story (to finish in the conclusion). Within a few sentences, though, transition to the paper's Topic, summarizing it (often a reading), providing background information for the audience, positioning the reader for your Thesis, the paper's main point. Ending the introduction (whether a single paragraph or more), the thesis stands out and leads directly to its proof, the first body paragraph. In this way, the essay's introductory paragraph (or two, even three, for longer essays) offers a progression of content ordered logically for the reader.

"They're here!"

Anna was looking out the back door, looking sweet, her hair light and long, and Digger moved quietly but quickly from the kitchen table to see the two little cats, dubbed Shyla and Skittles, who had graced their backyard since the past early summer.

The four pairs of eyes touched and started communicating, separated by two thin panes of glass, by the glow of civilization and the darkness of instinct. The magic of life gleamed in Digger's and Anna's eyes, hope and openness in Shyla's golden marbles, distrust in her sister's oval slits, for Skittles still seemed to hold a grudge about the spay-and-release treatment from early August, especially about that plastic head cone that she had so raged against that Digger had torn off the Velcro straps after just one day to stop her writhing and banging into fences and bushes.

"They're hungry," said Digger.

"Duh!" said Anna, not because she was calling her husband a dummy, but because they both hated when people used that expression and did so to laugh and to share an opinion.

"Duh!" said Digger back, and the two people laughed. Digger was glad to hear Anna's happiness because she had been closed up lately. He had decided to talk to her about it soon, maybe tonight during dinner or after. He gazed back at the pair of young cats, who stared back expectantly from beneath one of the dying backyard bushes (too much salt in the soil?). Shyla's eyes closed slowly and opened wide again, and Anna said, "Did you see that! Shyla just kissed us with her eyes."

"I saw it," said Digger, feeling happy and rightly placed, kissed by a little cat and by life. "Too bad Skittles won't do it."

"She's just not made that way," said Anna. "Just like some of my special-ed kids, she's just broken." Digger thought of his wife's absentee father, who might just as well have died as deserted her, and of her self-centered mother. *How was Anna made?*

"We can fix her," said Digger, and the four sets of eyes glowed back and forth, Skittle's frozen, slitted, like a reptile's eyes. Shyla rubbed against the trunk of the almost leafless holly bush.

"They want to eat," said Digger, and he went to the cupboard, pulled out a sack of dry food, reached back in for a can of wet, and put together a couple bowls of food. When he opened the back door, a cool breeze pushed in, along with the slap and shoosh of the waves, an attenuating lament of a gull, an emotional line through the sky. Keeping her eyes locked on Digger, Shyla half turned her body, and Skittles slunk back a few feet to stare from beneath another shabby bush, a rhododendron. As Digger descended the back porch steps, Shyla darted to her sister, and as Digger placed the two bowls on the bottom step, both cats leaned forward a bit. This was the closest to the cottage that he had laid the bowls. While at first he had put them under the farthest bush out back, twenty feet from the door, gradually Digger and Anna had drawn the cats closer, and now the feral felines were on the edge of civilization.

"Tsk, tsk," Digger called from the steps, and "Tsk, tsk" said Anna from the open doorway. Neither animal moved, however, until Digger retreated to the house and closed the door.

"They still don't forgive us for capturing them and taking them to the vet's," said Digger.

"It's hard to get over some experiences," replied Anna, and Digger thought, *Like what? Like your parents?* However, instead of asking, he just watched the two cats, Shyla first, slip from the skeletal bush and approach the steps in a series of dash and stops. When Shyla reached the bottom step, she began to wolf the food down, seemingly forgetting about caution, and almost immediately Skittles did the same thing. With every bite, though, the latter looked up at the doorway, prepared to flee. Digger wanted to soften the scared cat.

"I like to watch them eat," said Digger. "I wonder if parents feel like that when their kids are scarfing down dinner."

"Probably they're not approving," said Anna. She had obviously not had the best of luck when it came to parents. When she was just a little wide-eyed girl, her father had left his wife and only child, never to return. A child of divorce. Worse yet, according to Anna, she herself was the reason, at least that's what Deena, her mother, had said: "Your father just wasn't ready to be a father." As though the somewhat flashy woman were ready to be a mother! What parent would tell his or her children that *they* caused the separation? If Digger hated anyone in the world, it was his mother-in-law for what she had done to her daughter.

As the little cats ate, their black backs did appear to soften a bit, to sink into the ground, perhaps relaxed a tick by the aura of love surrounding the gift and security of food. The married couple watched the two feed as the sun began to slip down. It had been a dark day capped by thick, swirling clouds and gradually cooler breezes, colder than the previous summer-rimmed afternoon, this one an early October day that whispered "winter." Anna had once called October the most bipolar of months, stuck between summer and winter. Even November could be a mental weather month in New England, any month really, but Digger agreed with his wife about October, which would whisper winter dreams to him of snowfall. As twilight fell, Digger could see lacey whitecaps all through the bay, and he was glad to be inside, glad to be home all night with Anna, glad that she had not announced any sudden outings with Carrie, as she had been doing of late. Her best friend from college, Carrie had divorced her husband the previous year, and Digger had lost touch with Matt, her ex. For a handful of years, Carrie and Matt had been Digger and Anna's closest companions. Good times.

Shyla was just about finished. She raised a paw, licked it a couple times, and looked up the steps, blinked both eyes. She was thanking the humans and waiting for her sister.

"It's nice to be loved," said Digger, but Anna just watched the cats as though she had not heard. Maybe she hadn't.

Shyla was licking her muzzle now, raising her head to get further with her pink tongue, her white bib standing out. Both cats were female, small (nutrition deprived as kittens?), and black dipped in white, each having four white socks and a white belly, but only Shyla's white fur extended up her neck to her chin, reaching up to touch both sides of her nose, creating an inverted heart on her face.

"Look at Shyla's bib," said Digger.

"She's a proper little girl," said Anna, and Digger wasn't exactly sure what his wife meant.

"Why 'proper'?" he asked.

"Dressed for dinner," Anna replied.

"Oh," said Digger.

"Time for our dinner, too," announced Anna, adding "What are you cooking!" That was another of their shared jokes—Anna's lack of domestic skills. Digger didn't have too many of those either, so their cottage could look a little sloppy at times. *Most of the time.* But they had few guests these days, now that Carrie and Matt had split for good.

Digger picked up the empty cat tin and said, "Well, we're out of Savory Salmon, so how about spaghetti?"

"Do we have any veggie meatballs?"

"Yum, veggie meatballs. I think we do."

"Good," said Anna, a bit of a health nut. She had given up red meat long before their marriage. She had also stopped Digger from drinking coke and other soda, substituting ice water instead, so he always included her by putting ice in a second glass for her, even when she was not home. Lately, he had found many glasses a quarter filled with warm water on the kitchen counter overlooking the back yard.

Out back, Skittles was done with her salmon, and the non-winking cat didn't wait around licking and eye kissing. She slunk off fast, like a lost memory, thanking Digger and Anna only by finishing her bowl completely. Digger often didn't even need to clean the cats' bowls; the wild felines wiped them themselves.

He got going with their own dinner now. Anna had left the room; he didn't know what she was doing. In the past, Digger would walk into the bathroom to find his gray towel intertwined on the rack with her gold one, like a pair of mating boa constrictors, and sometimes Anna would cross her toothbrush with his, like a couple of cuddling giraffes, and just about every day they would "hair" talk, in other words, send messages on the shower wall with a few of Anna's long, light hairs, such as hearts (the first message Digger had created with a single Anna hair), or dog heads, or cats (previewing Shyla and Skittles), or bunnies (which would appear statue-like in their back yard and then disappear just as suddenly), or even words like "LOVE," and once Digger had been able to say "I love you" with a single fallen strand.

That sort of love endured, thought Digger, putting a pot of water on to boil. Love like that created energy that would blaze through any darkness, that would never flicker out. He trusted Anna completely, and he thought of that foundation as he clicked open the Prego marinara sauce and poured a little over half the bottle into another pot. When Anna had wanted to elope, he said *good*; when she had not wanted children, he said *great*; when she left dishes in the sink, he said *fine* and did them himself.

The fake meatballs were frozen into a clump in the bag, so Digger banged it on the counter. "Just banging the meatballs!" he yelled, but Anna was beyond hearing. Digger thought of hearts made out of hair and realized that those messages had not been sent in months, maybe a year or more. Anna rose earlier than he did now that he no longer taught eight a.m. classes, and when she took her shower, she no doubt had work on her mind. Her special-education classes were stressful, he knew. He had more mind work now, too, more responsibilities, more committees, more students to advise, more lesson plans to create, more papers, always papers. Life had become fuller, more plot oriented, and the little things had dried up, blown away. Adding olive oil to a frying pan, Digger suddenly realized that what he wanted the most right now were the little things, lots of small joys. Glad that the weekend had arrived, Digger just wanted to live—and to love Anna, along with the two little cats, the wind, and the waves. To love, he thought with a little glow, was to live.

As they ate the spaghetti, a quieter dinner than usual, Digger decided not to talk to Anna about her distance, to let the troubles play out. Anna would confide in him when she wanted to. He had accepted her secretive nature just as he accepted everything about her, knowing that her own parents had not been great role models, that her father had been aloof (then absent), her mother spoiled, even childish, telling the little Anna not to tell her father when her mother secreted home clothes and jewelry. Anna's mother had wanted a friend more than a child; perhaps she had actually wanted a mother herself. Deena certainly acted that way now, every statement to Anna (and to Digger, mainly on the phone) a missile aimed at the lake of guilt bubbling beneath life's surface, at least existing for children and no doubt for parents, too. Digger's own mother could shoot those emotional guns, but Jean Diggerson had a fuller life than Anna's mother seemed to live.

With dinner and after it, too, Digger and Anna drank white wine, moving out to the porch until the cold winds drove them inside to the couch. They had kept the TV off and just listened to the wind, always a presence for people who lived on the coast.

That night, they held each other in bed, communicating without words, those false messengers, and slowly explored the other with fingers, hands, gently and consciously at first, and then with less thought and more abandon. They melted, and for a short piece of time, the two humans fell out of this world completely.

Afterwards, they lay silently, and Digger realized that Anna had fallen asleep. He could not remember the last time they had made love, and he thought, "We've become old." Still, the physical connection calmed him, settled him. *I've become October*, he thought. *Teetered on the edge of sunny and sad.*

Later, Digger awoke in the darkness and felt extremely alone, but Anna lay beside him, turned away. Tipped into shadowy sadness, he stretched slowly out of the bed, went to the kitchen, and peered out into the darkness, wondering about his emotions. He could see nothing. He wondered if Shyla and Skittles were sleeping in the converted dog crate that he had wedged behind one of the spindly bushes, filling it with old shirts and little blankets, one floppy pillow. Gradually, the darkness beyond the windows lightened due to Digger's not switching on any lights and to a half-moon perched beyond the drifting armada of cumulous clouds, and the composition instructor saw ripples of white lace on the bay and listened to the whispering wind. *What did it say?* Digger felt alone but enlarged, that solitary feeling a person gets when the world's wonder and weight push down, magnifying perceptions and emotions, clarifying squeaks and whispers, casting thoughts toward the twinkling stars, moments that cannot be sustained for long and then end in the ego, a pinprick of thought drowning in meaninglessness and boredom. From the dark, into the dark, Digger had to admit that he felt change coming, and he didn't like change.

Chapter Three: Narration

As an organizational tactic, narration is not used often in a college essay since most papers deal with facts or with opinions supported by facts, not with stories (unless in the form of very short illustrative evidence). Sometimes, a brief story works well to begin an essay, especially when the student finishes the tale in the paper's conclusion, thus providing an interesting bookending strategy. In fields such as Education, a paper involving observation and synthesis will offer narrative opportunities, and for those body paragraphs, the story must be broken down into distinct parts (the skeletal plan) and developed with specific details (show; don't just tell).

After waking up that Saturday morning around 8:15 and finding Anna gone again, Digger had processed papers online. For three years, he had not collected print copies of essays, instead having students submit their papers in their course's Sakai software site. Although most of his colleagues stuck to their known hardcopy system and closed their ears to his reasoning, Digger would never go back to print copies, partly because students often had trouble reading his poor handwriting, but mostly because the online submissions helped everyone. No longer did Digger lug home a stack of papers, which had always depressed him a little even though he had accepted that about half his job took place at home, doing papers. Now, he not only heard no excuses why students didn't have a print copy ready on time, but also could return papers much quicker. A paper submitted on Friday could be clicked back on Saturday, not on the traditional Monday in class, and Digger also discovered that by using Word functions, he could color-code his comments, putting ones relating to content (to paragraphing control) in orange, the typical grammar ones in blue. Students tended to confuse revision (paragraphing work) with editing (sentencing work), so the color differences provided another way to show them the different steps in the writing process. Online, the student's paper could not be lost, either, and the Sakai software could calculate grades, too—very helpful for a somewhat math-deprived writing teacher. Digger had realized that some changes he did like.

Periodically, as the morning lengthened and turned into the afternoon, Digger went to the kitchen to get or heat his coffee, to eat some oatmeal (another of Anna's healthy changes in his life), to grab a sandwich, to feed the frightened cats (twice as the time stretched out), to wait for Anna (she had left a note saying that she was visiting her mother—*strange!*), and to continue with the papers, ending up sending twenty back—an entire class. He would get to a second class tomorrow.

The afternoon wore on. Because Digger had set his mind on finishing one entire class of papers, he did, but the aches in his neck and back told him that he had sat for too long. He moved about the quiet, empty cottage, looking out windows and feeling restless, the joy at finishing a large clump of papers smothered by Anna's disappearance—the dark center of a silver cloud.

At 4:30 he looked out the back kitchen window again to find two little faces gazing up below the bottom step, and Digger's heart jumped a bit. This was another stage in what he called "the civilization of the cats," for Shyla and Skittles had never waited so close to the cottage. As usual, Shyla's eyes were bigger and more open, both physically and socially, but Skittles (eyes still narrowed, body hunched) waited right alongside her sister, like a pair of kids' slippers, heads for toes. The two cats now lived completely in their back yard whereas in previous months, the two had disappeared for long stretches, much longer early on. Back in the early summer, the black-and-white pair, looking almost like big kittens, not small cats, had appeared just beyond Digger's wooden gate, which led to the sea grass fringing the beach, and that's where Anna and Digger had fed them for at least a month—on the far edge of civilization. Then with each week the humans would deposit the food bowls (they left a permanent water bowl out near the gate) closer to the back porch, drawing the cats closer. *Soon*, thought Digger, winking slowly at the cat with the inverted white heart on its face, the little wild animals would munch away on the porch itself, a good thing for all with winter's approach.

When he opened the door, as usual both cats retreated with their bodies, watching the man over their turned backs, but Digger noticed that they didn't run quite as far. He talked to them and said, "Tsk, tsk. C'mere Shyla, C'mon Skittles. Dinner time!" Every so often, Shyla would answer in a single "Meooow!" While the cry could have meant "bugger off," Digger took it as a connecting call, and although he coaxed Skittles to imitate her sister, the wilder cat never made a noise, as silent as the blood barreling through arteries.

Digger watched the little cats eat and then thought, "Where *is* Anna?" He could hardly believe that she would spend an entire Saturday at her mother's since his wife often referred to her only non-absent progenitor as another one of her special-ed kids—as "me, me!" oriented as a baby bird.

At 5:30 Digger heard the crunch of tires on their sand-and-pebble driveway alongside the cottage, and he looked out to see Anna's little white Honda Civic. Years later, whenever Digger would pass a small white car, he would peek over at the driver but never find Anna, just an old man or woman, another reminder of time. That pitiless beast.

Anna came through the door drooping, tired, without enthusiasm.

"Hello," she said.

Digger was a little unhappy with his partner: "You didn't want me to go with you to your mother's?"

"I knew that you had papers," she responded, placating him somewhat.

"I did one whole class."

"More tomorrow?"

"More tomorrow." For a writing teacher, more papers always waited.

"I fed Shyla and Skittles," Digger said, trying to forget about tomorrow, and Anna perked up a bit, raising her chin and looking at him as he spoke. "They came half an hour ago, and they were waiting just below the porch steps, right where we fed them last night."

"Another step in their civilization, right!" said Anna, and she smiled, too. The cats brought one of those little joys that life offered if a person made just a little of the required effort. "Let's see if they're still here," she added.

"They won't be," said Digger, but he still walked with her to the kitchen and looked out the back door. Just empty bowls greeted them, but even that emptiness was satisfying. To have nourished two little souls. The sun was dipping already, the north-west horizon glowing pink.

"It's getting dark sooner now," said Digger, but Anna didn't seem to hear him. "No cats," he added. "They're curled up in their crate, dreaming cat dreams."

"About birds and mice," Anna said.

"About us," Digger responded, glad to have her by his side again. "Are you hungry?"

Anna said that she wasn't, that she ate at her mother's, that they had had white fish, cod, along with brown rise and asparagus. Digger loved asparagus, even though it led to pungent pee. "How's she doing?" he asked of Deena, Anna's mother.

"Same as always: lonely, needy, manipulative. She showed me some pictures of my father that I've never seen. She hides them. She acts as though he died, rather than just left us."

"I would have gone with you."

"I know."

Anna's low energy drained the cottage a bit, especially with the little cats no longer in immediate residence, so Digger switched on the TV and made himself a little supper, scrambled eggs and toast. He ate alone at the kitchen table with just the wind and mumbled voices from the television for company. At 6:00 he moved to the couch to watch the local news, and before the sports report, Anna came out of the bedroom ("getting ready," Digger had determined, but for what he did not know) and said, "Carrie called my cell this afternoon. She wants us all to go out for drinks tonight. You too. Do you want to go?"

Digger knew that "us" and "you, too" really meant Anna alone because her friend Carrie was down on men these days (weeks, months, years). Still, he appreciated Anna's inclusion of him, not completely sure of its sincerity. Picturing the three of them seated in a booth and tossing out negative comments about the other, Digger suddenly wondered what Anna would say in his own absence.

"I'm really tired," he decided and said, "all those poopers." He used that word jokingly to describe his students' work since "poopers" of course, sounded like "papers." Only a handful of those essays, at most, could honestly be described as *waste*, only the ones showing little effort. Digger had actually said "poopers" to show Anna that he felt okay about her going. He only half understood why he did what he did, but maybe that was more than most people.

"Okay," said Anna, and she withdrew to the bedroom again. Digger watched her leave the room, focused on her long light hair and the way it looked like a pendulum of sorts, swaying back and forth slowly, the rhythm of time. In their child-less relationship, the two adults had always done what each wanted to do, creating less resentments and responsibilities, so Digger was not bereft at being by himself. Both he and Anna were at home with solitude. In fact, with only Anna did Digger feel that sense of timeless security that being by himself manifested, and for that reason, he knew that Anna was his spiritual kin, his soul mate. He derived his foundation of trust mainly from that connection, along with the fine wall created by two loving parents, a sibling (his sister, Emma), and a mainly happy childhood. And with genes, too, the simple luck of the draw.

Anna left as the nightly news ended, both watching the final story, about a little black boy who had founded a reading club. "I love reading," the ten-year-old beamed to end the clip, and Anna said, "That's beautiful." Digger had a little lump in his throat, too, and he thought of Danny Jones, of whether *that* little black boy had ever beamed like the one on TV.

By himself, Digger watched an old sit-com, had a beer, and then half followed a cops-and-robbers show that in the past had been decent enough. American TV killed with impunity. Nobody cared about security guards or passersby, all mown to earth without consequence to those tangential lives in the story. Down they went, the action passing them by. On to other scenes. Digger had another beer and went out to the back porch, sat on the top step, listened to the waves, to the wind, to the stars even. Twinkling abundantly beyond the gray fur balls and tattered pillows of passing clouds, the stars seemed to exude high, thin sounds, a chorus of pre-puberty boys, angelic. Digger imagined himself as such a boy, gazing up to spot fireflies, to catch the light and drop it in a big bottle. The stars looked a little like those long ago lightning bugs.

On this Saturday night, Digger's neighbors to right and left seemed to be out. He could see the soft arms cast by both front yard lights, but out back all the properties were black and silent. The sea called for it, for the darkness of mystery, or vice versa. "Shoooooooosh!" whispered the water, one breath rolling upon another, and Digger thought that if one word symbolized life, at least his, it was that continual admonition for peace and quiet. From his cottage, the lights of the Bay Bridge (spaced out along the rising, falling, rising, falling suspension cables) were blocked by a left turn in the bay, and he often wished that they weren't. That bridge was both lightness and dark to Digger, representing mankind's potential to create a wonder and his inability to control it: Poseidon's bursting from the sea. Perusing the shadows for cats, not finding them, he returned to the cottage's warmth.

By ten, he began to think of the late-night news and to wonder when Anna would come home. He was hungry again, scrambled eggs being a poor dinner. At 10:14 Digger decided to get a pizza, to surprise Anna (she loved pineapple on it) since she would probably come home with the munchies, so he called their favorite place, Mario's over the bridge. Then he thought of beer breath, although he'd had just two Buds over four hours, and brushed his teeth just in case. Then Digger went out the back door to his little truck. When he switched the headlights on, he saw a flash of black zipping into the dog crate and thought of Skittles, or maybe it had been Shyla, drawn by the sound of the door. When he returned, he would see if the two wild felines wanted a late-night snack.

The roads were quiet, too late to be out for older people, too early to head home for younger ones, and Digger felt happy being out in the night. From his dashboard, the lights created a little cone of security, a capsule traveling through space. As he glided through the curve that rose up and over the Bay Bridge, Digger glanced up at the string of lights and thought of the dark infinity above and of the dark finiteness below. He had once read that the suspension bridge, built during the depression, rose almost three-hundred feet into the sky (at its twin shoulders) and that the pavement itself hovered half that distance over the bay's swirling waters, fed by the incessant river to the north and the mysteries of the ocean to the south. The lights offered the bridge's surrounding neighborhoods, one encompassing Ocean View College itself, a continuous Christmas atmosphere. *Not always a happy and spiritual mood for some, though*, thought Digger as he passed the first great shoulder, feeling the winds pushing and pulling at his pick-up. Every year or so, a person jumped from the Bye-Bye Bridge, even students, he had heard (but none that he knew of in his seven years at OVC). After each event, publicized mainly in the local papers, arguments arose concerning suicide barriers, such as fencing or nets that would extend beyond a human's capacity for self-destruction, but then the debates died down, smothered by time and by logical points dealing with finances and aesthetics, the latter being a hidden point about money, too, the luring of tourists.

As the vacation destination of Bayside greeted Digger on the far end of the bridge, he remembered a fact that had stuck in his mind: Since the erection of the Golden Gate Bridge, some 1,600 Americans had used the monument to solve all their problems. That was about the entire winter population of Ocean View, and Digger imagined all those residents marching like ants, or lemmings, up the bridge, past the first soaring pylon, and off into the wild blue yonder. Recognizing the maudlin image, Digger pictured instead the pineapple pizza, the hot, gooey cheese, the soft crust, crispy on the edges. Mario's put more sauce on its pizzas, and that's why the pies were so delicious. Anna and Digger rarely went anywhere else for Italian food.

Mario's appeared just a mile up the main street, which on this end was fairly deserted since the bars didn't pop up until the road curved toward the Atlantic. At the pizzeria, Digger was the only customer, and the two workers, one girl and one boy (probably OVC students, but Digger didn't recognize them) were seated and looking bored when he entered.

"Quiet night?" he said.

"Not earlier," said the girl.

"It will pick up after eleven," said the boy.

"Right when we want to leave," said the girl.

"Large cheese and pineapple?" said the boy.

Large cheese and pineapple. That was him, admitted Digger, and then he thought of his well-read mother and corrected himself: That was *he*. That statement didn't sound right, but he knew that the grammar was spot on, for whatever that was worth. Digger stopped his mind and said, "Large pineapple cheese," as though that were his name. After the quick transaction, he said "Good night" and "Your shift will be over soon" and went back out into the deserted night.

He imagined Anna's smile when he returned with the pizza to the cottage. "Pineapple!" she would announce to the cosmos. On the kitchen table, he had propped up a note: "Gone to Mario's—love, Matt." He had almost left off the salutation, but then quickly penned it in, not wanting to be a hurt baby and mirror his wife's recent rejections (as Digger viewed her reticence), other than that one brief bout of silent love making.

On the Bayside side of the bridge, the approach was straighter, so Digger's eyes focused on the narrow sidewalk that lined both sides of the pavement, like the side stripes of a great snake, a King Cobra, as it rose up and wound its way back down. The narrow paths on each side also made Digger think of bicycles because he knew that pedestrians were not allowed on the structure, which extended a bike path that supposedly connected the top of New England to the bottom, even further perhaps. As he drove up the bridge, the suspension cables' lights, lower on either end of the mammoth construction, whizzed past the top of his vision, like madly flashing falling stars. At the top of his climb, the long stretch between the giant's broad shoulders, Digger did what he always did, day or night: He glanced to the right (up the bay) and to the left (out to sea) and felt one part wonder, one part possibility, and a smidgen of fear. Then his little truck passed the halfway point and soon would begin to nose down toward Ocean View.

Up ahead, off to the right, Digger saw something flap on the bridge's railing, which stretched several feet up, most likely to deter jumpers, Digger had always thought. The flap made him think first of a flag or maybe a plastic bag on its way to the galaxies. He slowed immediately, and when he saw the movement again, he realized with horror that a person was perched atop the railing just ahead, a person whose coat was flapping in the wind. No headlights approached, no help, *but what was that?* Digger imagined that down in the shadows of the bridge's descent he could see dark hoods, a little troop of people, and he pictured Bilbo Baggins and his trail of dwarves heading off into the wild. Through his mind, Tolkien's wondrous world often washed, but then the image vanished completely. Checking his rearview mirror, Digger saw no cars coming, just the bridge's falling lights, so after searching his lit dashboard for the emergency blinkers switch, he remembered where it was and clicked them on. The golden lights blinked in earnest into the darkness. Digger felt a punch of wind and heard its muffled roar. He was frightened.

But what about the jumper? How did he feel out in that tempest? Digger pushed open the drivers-side door and was attacked by the wind. It ripped the door wide and shrieked, blasting through the car, nudging and jimmying the pizza box, and toppling logical thoughts. Then it died, flew off, leaving a gulf of silence that was, if anything, even louder up here on the top of the world. Digger crawled out and felt the ground sway, but when he looked up, all motion stopped.

Clinging to the railing, his arms wrapped around the metal like one of those pathetic rhesus monkeys from those horrible psychology experiments, was a young black man. He had chosen a shadowed spot between the suspension cables' cascading lights, which left patches of dim illumination along the roadway, and for an instant Digger thought that perhaps just the shadows made the man black.

"Don't jump!" Digger yelled because he could think of nothing else to say or do, and the perched man looked down at him. His eyes looked as wide as the plates that held coffee cups, and just as white, too. With a start that rammed down his throat and just kept going, Digger recognized the night-distorted features of Danny Jones. For a second or an hour, Digger's senses deserted him—sound (the wind), touch (the pavement), smell (the sea), taste (the salt air), and almost even sight, narrowed to the student's face, to those frozen eyes. "Danny?" Digger said, but the wind jumped up and jammed the word back into his mouth.

From Bayside, headlights suddenly illuminated the macabre scene, Digger's gazing up, Danny's staring down, all the shadowed corners, the Van Gogh wind, and the approaching vehicle ignited Digger's senses again, especially the howling, slithering winds. "Danny!" Digger called. "Danny Jones, we can help you!" With "we," Digger was including the oncoming car, a four-door sedan, dark, but then the vehicle passed on by, a car full of college kids coming home early to campus. Digger glanced from Danny to the car repeatedly, seeing four faces aimed his way, recognizing none, willing the people to stop, waving both his arms. The faces looked distorted by shadow and by Digger's headlights, angular faces, hollow eyed, and for a moment Digger knew that they were dead, that everyone was, that they would offer nothing. The cascading cable lights from above provided only mood, just a touch of illumination, and the dark sedan descended down the bridge, taking Digger's hope with it.

"Help!" Digger had yelled to the faceless car when he realized that it would not stop. "Help! Help!" he called to its red tail lights departing, but the wind smashed his cries and threw them into the darkness: "Hell ... Hell ..."

The clinger's coat flapped above him, and Digger gave up on the vanishing car and its red, gleaming eyes. Looking up, he saw little Danny and the big gray hulks of swiftly sailing clouds and stars, stars, stars. A dark, beautiful night for a boy to fly. Danny Jones literally hung between being and whatever, if anything, was to come. "Danny! Danny! Danny!" Digger called, but the moaning winds tore the words apart and discarded the letters in all directions. All Digger heard was an echoing "Dam, dam, dam ... Ann, Ann, Ann ...ee, ee, ee ..." And Digger realized that he seemed to be calling for his wife, that in fact he was doing just that, calling for Anna, begging and raging. A little man, lost and helpless, on top of the world. He needed Anna.

That sudden clarity slowed Digger's mind, cleared the clouds, quieted the angry breezes, and he remembered from past reading that not all Bay Bridge jumpers achieved their goal, that some rose awakened from the water, swam to shore, and lived out their lives, that others floated half conscious until scooped from the bay with broken bones, twisted spines, the effects of the impact. How was that for an improvement on life! So high, so vulnerable, Digger did not understand how anyone could jump and live.

"Danny, you could hurt yourself!" But all Digger heard, and probably Danny, too, was "Urt, urt, urt ...," a seal's excited barking. "Please, don't! Please, don't!" And this time Digger heard that plea completely, loudly, like a whispered statement during a suddenly silent movie scene, because the wind had abruptly held its breath.

"I have to," fell the little broken voice of Danny Jones. In the sudden silence, this whisper seemed magnified.

"No," said Digger, sending the little word to the stars. "No, Danny! No problems are forever. Nobody's alone. No, no, …" Digger felt alone.

"They told me to," whispered the clinging boy who had failed composition class the previous semester. Had Digger heard those words or just read them from the boy's frozen face? *Who?* Then Digger thought of "They" and wondered if Danny had failed other classes.

"Nobody wants this, Danny. Nobody!"

"They do," whispered the boy, or at least that was what Digger heard.

And as if to prove the teen right, the winds screamed again, wrapping the two humans in sound and in fury, and in an instant Danny was ripped (*Did he rip himself?*) from the tall railing and just hovered in the sky. That was how Digger remembered it, like a snapshot almost, the severed cell from a movie reel, and then the following cells lurched ahead, and Danny was gone. Digger had not even seen him fall; Danny was simply no longer in the air. "Danny!" he said to nothing and to no one, and Digger's feet took him to the railing. Looking down, Digger realized again how high they were (he was), for far below he could see the rolling darkness by the glint of the stars' sorrow or maybe just by the bubbled breath of twisting currents. Danny no longer existed, nothing but darkness and the occasional flash of the moving beast, its eye opening to gaze up and see if Digger, too, would fall.

Chapter Four: Effect-Cause

This planning strategy should actually be called "Effect or Cause" since the body paragraph would be structured around either consequences (effects) or reasons (causes), not both, which would shift the topic halfway through the block of information. If the paper's topic were a problem of some kind, then a paragraph or more highlighting the effects of the issue would work to stress the need for a solution. Often, the ally's help a writer to generate consequences—i.e., financially, educationally, environmentally, etc. Any "ally" idea could then be broken into more specific effects, such as training, wages, expenditures, and profits for "financially," giving you plenty of manageable ideas to build your paragraph(s).

After the boy disappeared, Digger, like Danny, lost time. He wanted to run for help, to move, but suffered crippling inertia because humanity was so far away and because the air was so thick and dead, suffused with bitter salt, winds that whispered and roared, and pale pinpricks of light from empty stars. Ironically, 150 feet above the earth, Digger had never experienced nature's primitive underbelly so clearly, and he shrank from it, stood rooted to a ground that he could feel, the cold pavement of civilization.

He did not move until more headlights approached from Bayside, and this time the car stopped, right alongside Digger's truck, all the emergency lights blaring and creating quite a scene from shore, Digger imagined later. The loud lights belonged to a Bayside Police Department cruiser, one of which crossed the bridge hourly to stop what had just not been stopped. The Ocean View cops did the same, Digger discovered later. Sometimes, if one unit were early or late, the two cars or SUV's would pass each other, the officers' waving or saluting or at times even stopping side-by-side to converse, the way cops all over seemed to do.

Digger didn't hear the car stop or the driver's opening and closing the car door (probably left it hanging open), but then a big man, a big shape, stood beside him. They both looked down at the pushing-pulling sea.

"Did he jump?" said the shape, and Digger realized that the wind had closed its mouth again, that the sky was holding its breath. In his ears, Digger heard a high buzzing that he realized came not from without, but from within. Could cells scream? Platelets and neurons?

"Did you see him fall?" said the big cop again, taller than Digger, wider, with a nice voice, though, reassuring, not the commanding tone usually associated with police.

"He ..." Digger had trouble making a statement, forming words together. "He was just ...hovering."

The cop had a bright flashlight that bore through the darkness straight out from the bridge, and then the light shone directly down, the cop leaning over the lower rail's edge, and then straight up the massive girder that led to one shoulder peak. *Up*, thought Digger. *Where does he think Danny went?*

The cop told Digger a quick story: "One time, we had a reported jumper, and about ten of us were standing around this very spot. Ocean View officers, Bayside officers, even a pair of Statees, a real policemen's ball. Everybody taking a look down and doing nothing much else. Then somebody yells, 'He's up there!' Sure enough, we all look up to see that our fallen guy has actually climbed. Right up this pylon. About forty feet up. He's up there looking down at us like a treed cat. The firemen got him down with their ladder truck and a lot of luck. Craziest rescue ever."

Digger only half took in the tale, but the words, the human connection, soothed him, eased him down from where he was hanging suspended in space—not unlike Danny Jones for that instant—and set him on firmer ground. The cop was speaking to his own shoulder now, and Digger heard the abrasive scratching of electronic communication. The policeman had requested Bayside One and Two (*boats?*), along with the Coast Guard. "And contact Ocean View, too, Patty," the male voice commanded. Digger realized that he had not moved since Danny's fall (had just floated off for a bit), that he was still standing on the narrow bicycle sidewalk and facing north, gazing up the bay, the dark throat. The bay looked like a wide strip of black through a shadow land. But the throat would go the other way, Digger realized suddenly: Danny would be carried down, not up; he would be digested by the sea. Awakened by that truth, that acceptance, the composition instructor lifted up one leg a bit, then the other. His legs still felt like lead weights. He imagined gravity boots. He felt stuck to the bridge.

Two cars passed together from Bayside to Ocean View, both slowing down to see what was up, both being waved on past by the big officer and his powerful flashlight. Digger took in the beams as they illuminated the bridge's rails and cables, thinking of lightning and wondering where the wind had gone. He looked up to see nothing past the bridge's great skeletal reach, which from his view looked towering and almost unbelievable, like the Eiffel Tower, above which Digger saw stars twinkling, stars spread out across the heavens and blinking their eyes good-bye. He thought of Shyla and felt a ripple of concern. He thought of Anna and then of the pineapple pizza, of his note to her, her possible worry. He wondered where the gray clouds had gone, a whole fleet of them, and decided that the winds had taken them to other harbors. The macabre scene's details flowed through Digger like strong black coffee.

Soon, later, whenever, another BPD cruiser arrived, doubling the police presence. After the two cops reconnoitered, the new one being taller and thinner, the first walked over to Digger. He said, "You don't need to be here," not unkindly, adding, "but we do need a statement. The first on scene stays on scene, so Officer Marano will take you to the station and bring you back later for your car. You can get some coffee and warm up. If you're lucky, the donuts won't all be gone, but don't hold your breath!" Digger thought of the wind.

"Where's the wind?" he said to the cop.

"The wind's gone for now, but not for long, not up here." Then the wide man smiled and handed Digger a card. "My name's Myles, Special Investigations. You can call this number if you remember any details later. In these sorts of traumatic situations, often a person will remember details later."

Digger nodded and put the business card into his front pocket, neither man noticing that the little rectangle got stuck and then tumbled out, falling and bouncing from the bridge over the edge, spinning forever toward the water, landing in the wet over a minute later and floating eventually out to sea, following Danny.

Mumbling thanks to the policeman (*what was his name? Myles something?*), Digger let Officer Marano lead him to the back of a cruiser ("Watch your head." *Just like on TV*), and then he was pulled away from the dark bridge, gaining clarity with distance. By the time the car reached the BPD station, Digger was talking, leaning forward in the back seat to tell Marano what had happened and who it had happened to. "Danny said 'they' wanted him to jump, to die! Who's 'they'?"

"It's loud on the bridge at night," said Officer Marano. "The wind seems to blow louder in the dark." From his profile, Officer Marano looked young. Digger wondered how long he had been a cop.

"It *was* loud."

"Maybe you misheard," said the cop, and his voice was pleasant enough, too, making Digger think that Bayside must be a pretty nice place. He had mainly gone there for pizza.

"I don't think I misheard. Danny said, 'they;' said it twice."

"You can get all the details down in your statement. If someone or a group of someones assisted this Danny in a suicide, we will find out." Digger believed Marano. The streetlights flashed by, bright, blinding almost, reminding Digger of the bridge, of horrors hidden within shadows.

The lights at the BPD station were definitely blinding after the prolonged darkness on the Bay Bridge. Digger squinted and sipped the coffee delivered by Officer Marano, who with another cop—a female who looked older, especially when she addressed Digger (*must be her eyes*, thought Digger, and *those sunburst wrinkles*)—took his statement in a small back room. By the time he finished, the overhead lights had started to give him a headache. The two cops jotted down (on paper, not a computer) his personal information and then his memories: from going to Mario's (his reason for being on the Bay Bridge), to seeing Bilbo's dwarves or maybe so (he called them "hooded shapes" and "probably his imagination"), to spotting Danny Jones up on the railing, not recognizing him at first, seeing his fear, his not wanting to be perched up there (a conclusion that surprised Digger because he had not thought of it as the events played out), to the car that passed, to the four faces (male OVC students, he had thought), to his plea that they stop or at least call the police, to his feeling alone (he did not mention Anna) and helpless, to Danny's few and final words, his sudden jump (Digger mentioned the wind here and throughout his statement because its roar forever accompanied his memories of that night), Danny's appearing to stick to the sky, to disappear ("so fast, so suddenly!"). As he told his tale, the coffee grew cold, but it had helped him immensely, easing him down for once rather than lifting him up. Digger needed easing down. He thought of Anna, probably asleep at home, hopefully. Maybe she had read his note and was waiting at the kitchen table. He should ask for a phone and call her, but instead Digger just breathed, breathed, tried to empty his mind.

After his long statement, Digger wondered what the female cop's name was. He couldn't remember her having said it, but probably she had. On TV, cops always introduced themselves. Marano left the room, and with the little wrinkles around her eyes contracting, deepening, the not old/not young policewoman said, "If a 'they' talked that student into committing suicide, we will find out through social media—texts, Facebook, Snapchat, Instagram, just plain old emails. Young people write everything down electronically. No more diaries."

Digger recognized that the experienced officer was trying to make him feel better. He shook his head, partly because he didn't care much for social media and admittedly didn't understand it, and said, "But if you were racist enough or power hungry, whatever reason you had, if you tried to push someone to kill themselves, you wouldn't be stupid enough to leave an obvious trail, would you?"

The woman had a pretty face, just lined. She said, "Look at crooks. Half the time, they're so full of themselves that they film their crimes and post them on YouTube. And sell what they stole on Ebay. Social media has become law enforcement's best ally."

"I guess you know what you're talking about. I've heard that teenagers, young adults, have a part of the brain that isn't developed yet, the part that foresees consequences, that thinks things through."

The woman laughed shortly (*friendly Bayside PD!*) and said, "The criminals seem to be missing that part, too. Maybe you should do a study at OVC. You could compare the brains of crooks and college students."

Digger smiled. He didn't seem to have a laugh in him. "I'm not that type of professor. And I still have trouble believing that Danny's peers would leave a trail of electronic words if they had pushed him toward suicide."

The cop had an answer to that: "Young people do everything with their cell phones. You and I, although you're younger, Professor Diggerson, we turned in all different directions in our lives—to TV for news, to our parents for opinions, to the calendar for dates, to a landline for talking with friends, to clocks for time, to video games."

Digger caught on: "To cameras for memories. Twenty-four shots. And you took them to the pharmacy for 24-hour development, which seemed amazingly fast."

"Exactly. Well, kids today, and not just kids, even young adults—and older ones, too, it's catching—they go to one place, not all those others. They go to their cell phones. It's second nature."

"That's probably the first thing they see in the morning," said Digger, thinking of Danny's cell phone. It probably was in his pocket. Digger didn't want that image, the pocket at the bottom of the sea.

The cop continued her friendly argument, even though she had convinced Digger already: "If a group of students, any group or person, had wanted that young man to die, they would have taped it. They would have video-taped it on their phones. It would be on YouTube right now."

Digger thought of those dark hoods leaving the bridge. Had they been actual shapes or just the play of light and shadow?

"Those shapes that you saw, Professor Diggerson. If they had been real, they would not have left the scene. They would have stayed to enjoy and capture the show for prosperity."

Although the anonymous female cop was no doubt correct, Digger couldn't let go of Danny's words, especially the "they."

The station was warm, and despite the glaring lights and the thoughts that Anna might not be asleep, might be seated anxiously at the kitchen table raging at Digger for not getting a cell phone, he did not want to get up. He realized that he was being petty, punishing Anna for her recent lack of communication, yet he justified his inertia by telling himself that Anna was asleep, that calling her would just disturb his wife. He realized, too, that he feared going back to the bridge. However, he would have to do so because the female officer suddenly stood and told him that the young cop would return him to his vehicle.

The night air outside the station felt good, invigorating. It woke Digger up again. Officer Marano was less talkative now, probably tired, maybe nearing the end of his night shift. When they passed the pizzeria where Digger had purchased a pineapple pizza years ago, Digger thought, *So much for Mario's* because he realized that he would not be passing over the Bay Bridge anytime soon.

Except for now. From this south side, with the tall maples lining the road and flowing off into little forests, the bridge snuck up on a driver—peacefully narrowed pavement and overhanging trees and then suddenly a towering thing, an ascent. On the other side, Digger's side, the road swept up to the bridge, which could be seen long before the vehicle started climbing. On his side, a driver could be prepared for it, for climbing through the air. On this side, Officer Marano zoomed right up before Digger could stop him. What would he have said? *I don't want to go up there?*

Just past the halfway point, many police were gathered, their cars spread out and blocking the northbound lane. A couple cops with flashlights were directing traffic, one on either side, but there was little to direct. More cops strode about purposefully, tape was fastened to the crime scene (the fencing where Danny had perched), photographs blazed and died, and in the water at least three boats chugged silently with great cones of lights searching. Digger did not want to drive off the bridge; he felt small and scared, stupid. Only the stupid feeling kept him from asking a cop to ferry him to the earth and then deliver his truck down, too. Instead, he got inside the little Toyota, waited for the police to move aside and open a path for his descent, and then motored slowly down the bridge. This time, he didn't look left or right, just straight, and when he exited the bridge on the long gradual curve, he pulled to the side of the road, his hands shaking, and cried softly, cried for Danny Jones and for being alone. Cried for life's loneliness, its fragility. After that release, Digger wanted to connect to normal existence, so he opened the pizza box, touched the rounded crust—cold and hard—and thought of life again.

Driving home after midnight, Digger discovered that the world had changed, become deserted and alien. The lights were on, but nobody was home. Guilt dribbled into his mind, for he should have called Anna. *Would she even have answered?* When he pulled into his driveway, he felt relieved to see Anna's white Honda, and as he parked alongside it, he heard the stones and sand hissing quietly beneath his wheels. Before his headlights dropped into darkness, he saw a little black head with an inverted white heart peeking around the corner of the dog crate out back. A warm familiarity centered Digger just a bit. "Tsk, tsk," he whispered into the dark. "You want a snack, Shyla? Skittles? Hold on." His words sounded forced, a weak attempt at control.

Unlocking the back door, he entered a darkened cottage, cold with silence. Anna had left the living room light on, or perhaps he had. Perhaps her car was an illusion and she wasn't home again. Digger moved quietly to the bedroom and peeked (like Shyla) through the door, just ajar. Because their front yard lantern bounced off the side fence before succumbing to the night out back, Digger could see vaguely into the room: Anna was asleep, lying curled a bit, and the traumatized man felt a surge of something good. He *was* home. The shadows lost their grip and flapped off like disappointed crows. Most of them. Then a ripple of annoyance swept Digger, who had felt guilty about not calling Anna. Fast asleep and peaceful, she clearly had not needed the call, but beyond this quick flash fire, Digger mainly felt relief, though—rooted and safe.

At the kitchen counter, using only the soft light from the adjoining room, Digger added a little scoop of dry cat food to two bowls, topping each with some canned Seafood Delight from the refrigerator, and when he crept outside onto the back porch, the two wild animals were waiting below the steps, small black-and-white statues. Shyla had one paw up on the bottom stair. Moving slowly, not saying a word, Digger laid the bowls on the third step, one from the top, and neither cat dashed off during this new maneuver. Perhaps the dark soothed the wild animals, just as light buoyed humanity. Inside again, he saw that Shyla had already climbed two stairs and begun to eat with lunging mouthfuls, *quite uncivilized.* She had both front feet propped on the third step, one each around the bowl. Following her sister, Skittles kept half-closed eyes on the door, and in the darkened kitchen, the human wondered if the creature could see him. Shyla glanced occasionally at the door, too, but focused mainly on her food, rapidly disappearing. Anna would love this, yet if he woke her, the cats would be done and gone. All Anna would see would be empty dishes and darkness, and Digger suddenly pictured the Bridge, saw Danny clinging, the railing, the pylon disappearing into space, the cables casting down soft light, the stars, the wind whipping and snaking and snapping, making a mockery of Van Gogh's imagination. These horrors, the cottage and the cats had momentarily driven away, and Digger closed his eyes and shook his head quickly until the two cats returned to sight. After the bridge, the lights at the BPD station, the cops, their questions and their coffee, after it all, the cottage's solitude seemed unreal, not vice versa.

To flip those perceptions, Digger left the kitchen and flopped onto the couch. He thought about waking Anna but didn't move. She would listen in the nice way that she always did, an honest listener, and she would understand what he had gone through and offer honest empathy, just like she gave her special-ed kids. *She gave too much.* Digger let her sleep. Until the morning, he would save her from the awful reality of a student's suicide, from the horrors in his head.

Somewhere within the night's hushed passage, Digger slumbered, too, but if a lack of twitching and turning indicated a restful mind, then he did not achieve that state. He awoke to hear Anna in the kitchen: the "urrrrp" of a chair leg dragged, the gurgle of coffee rising. *Anna!* When he entered the kitchen, she turned and smiled, and Digger thought, *My Anna is small and beautiful, a ray of light that I can hold in my hands!*

She said, "I couldn't stay up and wait for the pizza, Matt. Sorry, I was beat. Where is it? You didn't eat the whole thing?"

Anna wasn't mad; she just didn't want him to consume that much cheese. Where was the pizza? *The pizza! Danny and the Bridge!* And the night closed in on Digger again, settling like a thick mist, cold and clammy. "I guess I left it in the truck." He walked over and kissed her tousled hair, and she squeezed his arms.

After she said, "I've never know you to leave a pizza in your truck," Digger didn't quite know what to say, how to explain it all, how to start, so he responded, "The cats greeted me. They wanted to eat." The subject of the cats was safe, seductive.

"I saw the bowls on the third step," said Anna, the light Anna again. "I just fed them there again, but they're gone already now. Maybe tonight we can coax them to the porch itself." She sounded like his wife again, and Digger thanked Shyla and Skittles for their existence.

"Soon, we can pet Shyla," said Digger, and he thought of her big round eyes, then of Danny Jones' with the stars all around him. The image closed his lips.

"You want coffee, Matt? I brought the paper in. I hate to tell you this, but an Ocean View student jumped off the bridge last night. They couldn't find him, either, at least not by the time the paper went to press. It's on the bottom of page one. What's wrong, Matt?"

Apparently, Digger's face had done something strange. It certainly felt frozen. He opened his mouth. "I was there," he said, and Anna made an emotional noise. "The pizza," he added and saw that Anna understood, that she had pictured Mario's beyond the bridge. "I saw him fall. I knew him. I tutored him last semester and just ran into him at school yesterday, I mean Friday. His name was Danny Jones. He was very quiet, didn't seem to have friends. Last semester, he failed his writing class with the Grammar Nazi, and this semester he had Paul Smith. Imagine that? He was black, is black. Danny was African-American. I was with him." And then he concluded, "I left the pizza in my truck."

As Digger blabbered these facts, Anna had moved toward him and touched his arm, his shoulder, and Digger thought, *Anna's come back to me. Wherever she moved off to, she's back now!*

His wife made Digger sit, brought him coffee, toasted an English muffin and split it with him. Just as he had done with her, she was waiting for him to release anxiety, to tell her what he had to communicate, to unleash. Leading him off the bridge for a bit, Anna looked out back for the cats, announced that they were both gazing out the back gate, and then showed him the paragraph from the Sunday paper, the only one they subscribed to because they didn't have time to read so much during the week (Anna got her news mainly online, Digger most often from the TV) and because the couple liked to spread the big Sunday paper out and read it leisurely throughout the long weekend day—except when Digger had essays to check online (far too often!). The paper's blurb didn't say much, just that an "unnamed" OVC student had jumped from the Bay Bridge between 10:30 and 11:00 Saturday night, that this student was "missing and presumed dead," and that the suicide had been witnessed by an OVC professor, also "unnamed."

"I'm unnamed," said Digger.

"That's good," said Anna as she topped off his coffee. "It's usually not good to be named in the paper."

Digger thought of people named in papers, of crooks and corpses. Nodding, he said, "This coffee's great. The coffee at the cop station wasn't so good. Weak and lukewarm, like tea." Digger made a face before continuing. "The lights were blaring. Weak coffee and strong lights—just the opposite of what we like."

Recognizing that he was blathering again, Digger continued nonetheless, telling Anna about the cops who interviewed him, the wide one and tall one, the one with starburst wrinkles, about social media and detection, about the deserted ride home, about the pineapple pizza and Mario's, not about the pivotal scene, though, not about Danny, his face and words. Digger did not want to relive those details, not yet, not even with Anna. *Why?* Maybe she would not be able to help, and in that event, Digger would be lost.

Before long, Digger lifted his body up and lost his thoughts in student papers online, Anna's occasionally breaking in to deliver coffee, some scrambled eggs (she could cook those, but tended to dry them out), some peanut butter on crackers. At one point, she must have gone to his truck for the pizza, and he somewhat reluctantly (associations!) ate a limp micro-waved slice. Realizing that Anna was being more domestic than usual, that she was concerned and wanted to help him, Digger felt stronger. *She can save me!* he thought. The papers, the snacks, the Sunday snail's pace, all helped to heal or at least cover a wound that Digger felt but could not find. Two wounds, he realized, for Anna's gradual withdrawal from him had created a thin tear within. He had been bleeding internally, down deep. For as long as he could remember, Digger had been aware of darkness within, not evil, not something that had to be caged, but a shadowed place rooted in his sub-conscience, just rippling above it, enough to be noticed, a whisper. He called this zone his black river, and in it he plunged all of his insecurities, frustrations, guilt, any dark emotion that threatened his waking, walking thoughts. Digger thought that everyone must have experienced a similar shadowed stream within, but Anna had said that she did not. Anyone else, Digger had never told or asked.

Between papers, Digger dipped into his black river, which ran high with the weight of Danny Jones, ran wild due to the whipping of those malevolent bridge winds, which refused to stay still or silent. Digger worked on, worked through, adding comments (content ones in orange, grammatical in blue, with green end comments summing up his suggested revision steps) to each digital composition, re-attaching it through the online site's Assignments link, and submitting the critiqued essay back to the student, one by one. His English 101 students were currently analyzing the language choices in a narrative essay dealing with the writer's visit to a slaughterhouse. A startling piece of non-fiction draped in rhetoric, it was an essay written by a surgeon (Doctor Richard Selzer) and used occasionally by Professor Matthew Diggerson, who wanted students to experience powerful prose pieces, to recognize the pen's potential. Selzer's article offered interesting metaphors, manipulative descriptions, and words slanted both positively and mainly negatively, given the harsh subject matter. In orange, he added comments like, "Which word is especially connotative and why?" while in blue, he suggested, "Check #1a from your SC—who does what?" The SC was his Sentencing Checklist of common grammatical problems, #1a covering weak-verb wordiness. Every new surge of students carried with it the old waves of problematic patterns, such as their writing too broadly and relying on passive verbs to build their sentences. From one semester to the next, Digger repeated this mantra: "Be specific!"

Around 2:30 in the afternoon, the teacher finished the 101 class' papers, checked his email, and then thought happily of football, a reward after the pile of work and the fantastic horrors of the bridge. For the last few essays, he had not heard Anna, and when he left the computer (no place to put it but the cottage's largest area, the living room), he found a note in the kitchen— "Gone shopping!"

Two words, darkness and light, "gone" and "shopping," the latter creating the hope that Anna would return with a sweet of some kind, perhaps just herself. *The Patriots later, too*, Digger thought, anticipating the 4:30 kickoff. *Some game must be on now as well*, and Digger clicked on the remote and switched to Fox, finding the Giants and Redskins, a match from Digger's youth, when every televised game involved the New York Giants and some Eastern Division rival: Eagles, Cowboys, Skins, or Cardinals, before their move from St. Louis. *Might as well root for the Giants*. Anna could not understand the gridiron's appeal, but for Digger football was beautiful, the runner's gliding past obstacles, the ball's arc through an autumn sky, a linebacker's missile-like collision into the thighs of a toppled giant. On this day, the Giants were being beaten by the inferior Redskins, who had done little winning since the days of Digger's childhood. The game was a little boring, easily haunted by a flying, falling boy.

Before the Pats game came on and more solidly drew his attention to the present, Anna returned. Digger, Shyla, and Skittles had all heard the sound of her tires, were all watching as she walked with a paper bag toward the back door, which Digger opened. As Anna thanked him and passed into the kitchen, Digger felt the ocean's cold breeze pass by, too (*the Boy on the Bridge*), and Skittles saw it as well, the cat's gold eyes narrowing, cutting the black vertical pupil in half. Under the sky's touch, the little cat scrunched, as though a hand had reached down and stroked her back. "It's okay, Skittles," Digger said. "It's just a shadow."

"A shadow?" Anna said.

"My black river rising," answered Digger. "Skittles can feel it, too. It must be connected to instinct somehow. Are you sure you can't feel the black river?"

"I'm too evolved," said Anna, but she was laughing, the words light, like flower petals, gold and silver dancing in the air. "Those cats are always hungry," she continued. "Just like you."

Digger laughed (the noise sounding hollow but feeling good) because he was about to say, "Just like you" even though it wasn't true. Anna ate like a bird, just pecking sporadically, sometimes even fasting for a day or more. On this Sunday, though, she had brought home an apple pie, half of one anyway, without sugar. As they ate at the kitchen table, Digger said, "How do they make a pie without sugar?" and he sifted a white frost over his slice.

"They make the pie but don't add sugar, I guess."
Anna said this without sarcasm, probably because she
had never made a pie. Neither had Digger, though. He
pictured the roundness and then Danny's eyes and then
the nebulous word "they," the shadows who wanted a
boy to die. *Who?* Peers? Family members? Teachers
who had failed him? Ghosts and goblins? Winds? He
could hear those winds now, the real ones sifting
through his back yard and the imagined presence
howling from the dark bridge. *Ghosts.* Digger accepted
that from then on he would be haunted. The coming TV
Patriots marched into his mind, too, and he welcomed
them. New England was on the road this week, playing
the Broncos in Denver. *Mile High*, thought Digger, and
for a moment up went his thoughts. He was glad to be
at home.

Why was he not telling Anna about "they"? Was it
because she had not asked him more about Danny? In
the past, they had not played games with silence. This
untrustworthy thought buzzed and bothered; Digger
wanted to kill it.

"This pie tastes great even without the sugar," he
said, his mouth full.

"Without the sugar! What's all that white stuff?"

"I see no white stuff," said Digger, smiling,
changing the subject. "How's Carrie? Still hating men,
Matt in particular?" When the two couples used to
socialize, Anna and Carrie had played a game called
My Matt, "Matthew" being both husbands' Christian
monikers, and it would go something like this:

Anna: "My Matt made me dinner."

Carrie: "My Matt didn't."

Anna: "My Matt likes to read."

Carrie: "My Matt doesn't."

If the two Matts were present, one would laugh
while the other grew gradually crimson and uttered

things like, "I read!" It was actually a good-natured game, one of acceptance seemingly, and Digger had always thought that his friend Matt had been silly to get defensive. As the years ran on, though, Carrie's Matt jokes grew darker and solidified, and nobody laughed or liked them, except for Carrie apparently, the mirth feeding something dark within her, something that hatched two years ago and ended a union. Digger had realized then that a successful marriage needed more than love, that *like* was crucial, too. Maybe his friends had loved but didn't like, or liked but never loved. He wasn't sure which, if either, but Carrie and Matt were missing the something that pushed strong couples past life's obstacles.

Anna seemed to be contemplating Digger's Carrie question. She forked up and dispatched her last portion of apple pie, chewed, swallowed, said, "She's much happier now. She doesn't even mention Matt. I don't know where he is or how he's doing." Then she let the other Matt's mysteries hover.

"Me neither," said Digger. The other Matt had once been his good friend, but without Anna's and Carrie's setting up social events, Digger had just allowed time to flow by. Finishing his pie, too, Digger realized that that's how he had begun treating life since Anna had drifted away a bit: He just let it flow by. With the expanded responsibilities and excitements of being a full-time faculty member, the committees and advisees, the research and peer reviews and occasional writing, life had to flow by in order for anything, everything, to get done. Even weekends like this current one brought more work in the form of papers, which built up precipitously if not processed almost at once. Digger had accepted these responsibilities with the promotion—the prestige, security, and larger checks— had experienced most of the work as an adjunct anyway, but had Anna accepted them, too? Her special-ed teaching demanded fewer actual hours but definitely more emotion. Digger's work required mainly logic and diligence.

The Boy on the Bridge. That image defied logic, yet there it existed, as fact. *They.* That antagonist haunted pathos more than logos (*right?*), for who would, who could, cause another person to step off this world? Digger would ask this question a thousand times a week, but he did not ask Anna, not yet.

Chapter Five: Sentence Planning

> *Writers must plan not only paragraphs, but also sentences, choosing a simple sentence to make one strong idea stand out, a compound structure to stress two equal thoughts (with an "and," "but," or "so" usually), a complex organization to show one main idea and one or more subordinate ones (using coherence-creating words like "because," "although," "when," and "if" commonly), or a compound-complex sentence type to juggle multiple related ideas, two standing out. To convey ideas clearly and coherently, you must determine the more important point(s) and structure even sentences accordingly.*

Two days after Danny Jones hovered (like an angel) and fell (like an angel, too), the BPD released the victim's name, and OVC administrators issued a campus-wide email of condolence, containing plans for a memorial later in October. The memorial would take place outside the library, a common gathering spot (when New England's weather cooperated) for any media-connected events, such as announcements or awards.

Still "unnamed," Digger had clammed up about his experience, partly because Anna didn't ask him about it (*probably didn't want him to relive the horror*). He wanted her to ask, but the concern had to come from her. Digger knew that he was being stubborn—and stayed that way.

The following Sunday morning, Digger felt Anna leave the bed (she was a morning person, not him. *What was he?*), heard her clanking around making coffee, listened to the front door creaking (she was getting the Sunday paper), and then sat up when Anna yelled, "Uh, oh!" She came fast into the bedroom, newspaper dripping in folds from her hands, and said, "They know it was you, Matt!" Confused momentarily, Digger felt hot guilt ("It was me!") and then cool comprehension.

"The bridge," he concluded.

"You're named," agreed Anna, reading "The previously anonymous Ocean View College professor has been unmasked, Humanities Professor Matthew Diggerson (33), a full-time faculty member." She looked from the paper to Digger. "Who could have said it was you? The Bayside police?"

"Unmasked?" said Digger, frowning. "That's not a very objective word for a hard news piece. I sound like the Phantom of the Opera, like I've got something to hide." Then he said, "Must have been the cops, but maybe my statement's a public record. Or maybe somebody in a passing car saw and knew me. A group of students passed by gawking. They didn't stop or help, though."

"You didn't tell me that!"

At this accusation, Digger felt annoyed, so he squashed Anna's statement, subordinated it out of existence, substituting a new point: "Coffee?" he said. To her credit, Anna dropped the accusation, too, and brought him a steaming cup—his favorite one, Kelly green like the Boston Celtics. Digger sat up, sipped the boiled brew, and gradually became human. Anna rarely saw him in the morning, and when she did (on weekends), she knew to leave Digger alone with his coffee for a bit. Although her husband was always good natured, he tended to respond in grunts and single words for about fifteen minutes each Saturday and Sunday morning. She called him "Caveman Matt" and accepted him, just as he had learned to live with her domestic incapacities. The longer he lived, the more Digger realized the importance of acceptance.

Half an hour later, at the kitchen table, Digger gave Anna the details of that night, a week past. She expressed continued surprise and repeated you-should-have-told-me's, and each time she did so, Digger held back his resentments, which he periodically drowned in his black river. Only once did he say, "We haven't talked as much lately," whereupon Anna nodded quietly, her eyes glazing over as her mind surveyed the distances. She was saved from a response by the telephone blaring from both the living room and the kitchen wall next to the back door. Digger got up and used the latter phone: "Hello."

"Matthew, this is your mother."

"Yes, Mom. I recognize your voice."

"Why didn't you tell me that you witnessed that boy's suicide? I nearly fell out of my chair when I read your name in the paper! What were you doing so late at night on that awful bridge?"

How easily can concern turn into condemnation. Knowing that Jean Diggerson meant well, Digger accepted (almost) that her habit was to express love through anxiety, that only he could make himself feel defensive, and that if he didn't say something, answering one of the questions, at least, then a fresh onslaught would ensue.

"Matthew, are you there?"

"I went to get a pizza," he said, squashing more defensiveness (a pattern this morning), even chuckling silently.

"Pizza? Right now?" His mother had never done well with sarcasm.

"Mom, last Saturday night, a week ago, not now. A week ago, I was on the bridge because Mario's, our favorite pizza place, is on the other side. It was only a little after ten, too. I was getting us a pizza."

Mom was just barely placated. "Well," she said, "What happened?" and Digger told her what he had just told Anna, leaving out some of the haunting details, though, such as Danny's big eyes and strange words.

"Did he say anything?" His mother should have been a reporter or a cop.

"He said that somebody wanted him to do it," admitted Jean Diggerson's son, and when she demanded, "Who?" he said that he didn't know, that he had asked that same question a thousand times since.

"Is Anna there?" His mother asked surprising questions.

"Of course," said Digger, wincing because he had vowed to himself never to use those two words, which in his mind dripped defensiveness or judgment or the bitter offspring of those two ugly forces. "She just made me toast," he added, and then, "She even put butter on it. Do you want to talk with her?"

No, she did not, not right now, and after demands to "keep me informed" and "call me," they hung up. After the call, the cottage seemed especially quiet, but ten minutes later the phone blared again.

"Your mother?" said Anna.

"Let's see," said Digger, rising again. The kitchen phone had an extra-long cord so that he and Anna could sit at the kitchen table while talking. Digger said hello.

"Jonathan Rockwell of *OV Weekly*," came the reply.

"You saw my name in the paper," said Digger.

"Sure," said the reporter. "We at your local paper wanted to be the first to get your views. You haven't talked with the daily, right? If so, they would have quoted you."

"You're quick," said Digger, looking at the nearly empty coffee cup and then at the pot, nearly empty, too. Anna had just left the room, and Digger didn't want to get up and make more. "Actually," he said into the phone, "you're the first reporter to call. Nobody from *New England Times* has contacted me."

"They will."

"Thanks for the warning." Then Digger thanked Jonathan Rockwell again by describing the bridge scene for the third time that morning, this time adding more details than he gave his mother but less than he revealed to Anna, partly because he wondered whether the cops wanted him to give details (they didn't in murders, but this was a suicide, right?). In the end, he did tell the reporter what Danny said, thinking as he did so what the headlines would be: "Who Killed Danny Jones?"

Rockwell stated, "The boy said 'they,'" halfway between a statement and a question.

"He said, 'they,'" repeated Digger. "Something like 'They want me to,' and then he repeated that idea when I told him that nobody wanted him to jump."

"So you talked with him, had a real conversation?"

"Real short," responded Digger, tiring, glancing at the coffee pot again. In truth, he could no longer remember exactly what Danny had said that night, although the full transcript would be in the Bayside Police Department files. The reporter asked a couple more questions (about Danny himself), which Digger answered as best he could, tiring of the conversation, adding, "That's about it, Jonathan."

"If I have more questions, I'll call back," said the reporter, and Digger noticed his lack of a question, his implied point about access to future information.

Reporters, thought Digger, an expert already after one experience.

"I won't be home today," Digger decided to add, and the reporter told him that he was learning fast. They both said good-bye. *Where was Anna? Where was coffee!*

The morning passed. Anna made appearances from the bedroom, but worked continually in there on lesson plans for the week. Digger had a rare Sunday off (no papers, no lesson plans, no articles to peer review, no committee work to research), so he watched two entire football games, plus the somewhat obnoxious pre-game show at noon (four laughing heads and some banal interviews with athletes). He had not had an open weekend like this since before the fall semester. He had time, he had space, he had nothing to do. It got a little boring. Once an hour or so, he listened to the phone call out for him, but he stayed on the couch except when going to watch for the cats, to feed them, to refill his coffee, or to stick some food into his mouth. Anna had long since closed the bedroom door.

As October shifted on its axis, Digger spent more and more time with his advisees, that is, with the two dozen or so students assigned to him in order to guide them through their four years (sometimes five!) at Ocean View College. With the spring semester's schedule available, registration was coming soon, so even Digger's class-less Tuesdays and Thursdays became busy with comings and goings, with names remembered and requirements for various majors checked. Digger both smiled and cringed over this advisee responsibility, one that he had not had as an adjunct faculty member. The advisees made him feel more "rooted" to OVC, to something larger than himself, and that foundation was very important. Most of the two dozen or so slightly anxious young students thanked him honestly for his help, sometimes requesting letters of reference for internships or for first real jobs upon graduation. On the other hand, the advisee meetings ate up time and energy, adding on to his already busy schedule.

In his classes, the lessons for both English 101 (analyzing non-fiction) and both 102 (focusing on fiction) classes dealt with editing since Digger would grade the second main paper soon. For 101, his students were analyzing the Selzer "slaughterhouse" piece, and for 102, they were studying Tea Obrecht's story called "Blue Water Djinn." Digger liked the author's magic-realism short stories better even than the master's of that genre, Gabriel Garcia Marquez. For these second projects, Digger stressed editing for coherence, having highlighted conciseness (clear subjects and active verbs) in September's first main project. Since the key to coherence was subordination, Digger had created an active, fun subordinating-practice exercise years ago, before his time at OVC even. He called this exercise Add-Ons, and in his first English 101 class (11 a.m., Monday, Wednesday, Friday), he explained what he wanted the three big groups, desks formed into circles, to do.

"For Project One, we worked on wordiness, on creating concise clauses, word groups with clear subjects and active verbs, like this." Then he wrote (with chalk since he was teaching in one of OVC's older buildings for his first two classes, both 101's) three words—"The dog barked"—on the dark green board. "Remember the 'who does what?' or 'what does what?' question? Now we're going to work on coherence, your flow of information, which requires coherence, in other words, subordinate clauses and phrases, both of which need to be connected to a main clause, like this 'dog' one, to create a sentence. Without subordination, you will stress too many main points and force readers to figure out which ideas are more important and how they relate. That puts too much pressure on your audience. You don't want to make them work; you want to lead them through your analyses. Okay, let's add some subordinate info to this base statement," and Digger turned again to the board's "dog" sentence.

At this point in the exercise, most classes would stay silent until the teacher prodded volunteers with questions like "Why?" and "Who?" But Digger's eleven-a.m.-ers were very sociable and outspoken. Mandy, the girl Digger had seen with friends on the most recent path-of-worms day in early October (before the fall), raised her hand and said, "Because the dog barked, I ran," and a few students giggled at that.

"That's a nice example of subordination, Mandy, but for this exercise I don't want to subordinate my main clause. I don't want to put 'because'—my favorite word, by the way, since most good writing tries to answer why—on 'the dog barked.' I want to keep that as my main clause, my statement. So I'll rephrase your example to show what I mean by stressing a point."

Then he turned to the board and scratched "Because I ran" before the "barked" statement. Looking from the students (none on their cell phones—*good!*) to his expanding sentence, Digger said, "See how I stress the *barked* point by subordinating the *ran* one? That's the key to coherence. Showing how ideas relate and stressing just the important point."

Another student, Michael (Digger usually had one or more Mikes per class) raised his hand and said, "I thought you couldn't start a sentence with 'because.'" Thinking that students had a tendency to get off focus, Digger said that he had been told that, too, and that he wasn't sure why, that "Because" was a great way to start a sentence since it implied how the sentence's ideas related, a logic connection, and showed which idea was more important, the statement after the "Because" word group. He ended by saying, "Those teachers probably wanted us to avoid a fragment since some students might put a period after the subordinate word group beginning." Michael nodded, as did a few others (Digger thought of bobble-heads, but not unkindly), and the add-ons modeling continued. Within a few minutes, Digger's little dog sentence looked like this:

"Because I ran across the back yard, the dog, who was tied up with a big chain, barked loudly, biting into my leg even though his name was Fluffy."

Digger had laughed with students at the "Fluffy" addition and had changed the "leg" one from a student's original suggestion of "butt." Now he underlined the subordinate word groups and queried the class about each, asking one question repeatedly: "Subordinate clause or phrase?" He wanted the students to remember what subordination was, what it looked like, knowing that grammatical knowledge could lead to sentencing-skills acquisition. Most students soon understood the difference between the word groups, that the opening that began with "Because" was a subordinate clause because it contained a subject-verb ("I ran"), and that the next underlined group ("across the back yard") was a phrase since nobody or nothing was doing or being anything (i.e., no subject-verb).

After transferring this knowledge, Digger had the three big groups (five or six per circle) apply it by beginning the add-ons exercise. First, he told students to write a base sentence—a short main clause like his "dog" one—in the middle of a piece of paper, a moment that always led to one or two students per group ripping out some pages from their notebooks since at least half the students no longer brought notebooks, just laptop computers. Then, after checking that everybody had not only a pen or pencil, but a workable sentence—birds flew, cars crashed, cats meowed, students smiled, etc.—Digger said, "Now, don't add me to any of these sentences since bad things tend to happen in them [students laughed]. Also, don't swear or add sex or embarrassing content, okay? Okay, now pass your sentence, clock-wise in the group, and add a subordinate structure, a subordinate clause or phrase, as we did on the board, to your peer's main clause. Remember, don't subordinate the main point, just add around it, and don't use 'and' or 'but,' because you'll end up with a long run-on sentence. Wait until everyone's added a subordinate word group, not an individual word, since we're practicing using subordinate clauses and phrases. Don't forget the beginnings of the sentences, too," and Digger pointed to the "Because" opening on the board's example. Many students repeatedly checked the board to get ideas or maybe to steal them.

"If you can't think of a word group," Digger said, looking at the clock over the board, just add, 'at 11:14.' That prep phrase will probably work in any statement. Okay, wait for everyone and pass again, clock-wise. Keep adding and passing until these sentences are full of subordination."

Even students who hated grammar (i.e., most students) liked this creative exercise because they were actively engaged and because the resulting sentences were often funny. In the third group (going left to right), Mandy looked particularly animated—confident, talkative, tanned, as though she spent a lot of time on boats (and probably did, her father probably owning a yacht or two). Digger let the groups work and then said, "When you get your original sentence back, add one more subordinate word group and that's it."

The groups tended to finish at about the same time, and Mandy's group started sharing the sentences and laughing before Digger gave more directions: "Okay, now read all the sentences, choose one to show the class, edit it if necessary, and write it on the board."

Watching the three groups functioning, Digger felt good, had not even thought of Danny and the Bridge (maybe just a flickering shadow here or there, a splash and trickle from his black river). The writing teacher loved to see groups focused on an activity, learning without even realizing it! *Planning and purpose*, Digger thought, *the keys to a successful lesson*. And within a few minutes, an emissary from each cluster had gone to the board to reveal the results of their efforts. Digger read the first two add-ons sentences as Mandy scratched her group's creation into view, the chalk protesting, making Digger flinch. The first two sentences went as follows:

"Because it was hungry the cat, which was fat, and had a hat, meowed running away with the spoon, the cat jumped over the moon."

"Filling the sky with white balls of puff, at 11:14 the clouds sailed by, making me wish for the sun, because the day was cold at 11:14."

The day was cold, Digger thought, along with, *I need to do more comma work.* And he laughed inside at the repeated prepositional phrase ("at 11:14"), but not at the comma splice (*pesky run-ons!*) in the first sentence. As Mandy finished her group's chosen example, Digger said, "For your presentations, just read your sentence aloud to hear if it sounds right. Mistakes can sneak in when you're adding so many word groups. Then break down the word groups and tell us if each is a subordinate clause or a phrase. Know the difference so that you can analyze your own sentences."

As he spoke, Mandy moved back to her group, and when Digger turned to the third sentence, he read this:

"Because he was quiet, never asking questions or joining in, Danny jumped off of the bridge at 11:14 in October because the Goths told him to."

Digger was stunned into silence, as was the class— whether by his frozen stance or the sentence itself. *The Goths? That crow-like group of students?* Digger remembered having seen them behind Danny that day near the Admin Building. Had they—"They"!—caught up to him? Badgered him? Planned his death and executed it? He remembered Danny's eyes and then Bilbo's dwarves, that clustering of hoods that Digger imagined leaving the bridge that night. *Just shadows? Just ghosts?* The ghosts of all those who chose to depart via the Bye-Bye Bridge. Then Digger's mind shifted to the newspaper yesterday, to his being named. Did *they* know he was there? His students weren't moving, weren't taking the opportunity of silence to look down into their laps at text messages or at videos of high school boys crashing skateboards. That thought brought Digger back to the Goths. *Non-conformists.* He had one of those black-clad members in his late class, a fellow named Josh (*lot of Josh's in his classes these days*).

Digger returned to reality, or at least to the present. The clock read 11:43, and because he realized that the groups would have no time to present these three sentences, Digger went through each one quickly, identifying the subordinate clauses (the "because" and "which" word groups), the phrases (he especially liked the descriptive verbal "ing" ones in the second sentence), adding and deleting some commas, fixing the run-on in the first sentence by changing the last word group to "the cat's having jumped over the moon." No questions ensued (the students were eying the clock, too), so Digger told the class to "dial up" their language papers and to look for adverb clauses, for words like "because," "when," and "although."

"You want to use a lot of these words," he advised, adding, "Check to see if you use them," and then suggesting more words to look for and/or to use: *since, if, while, after, once.* "Use plenty of these words," Digger repeated, "because adverb clauses really create coherence, showing how two ideas relate, by logic, by time, by contrast." Digger kept talking, repeating the words and the reasoning, as students scanned their essays or pretended to.

"Okay," he concluded. "That's it for today. Your papers are due for a grade on Friday, so be sure to edit for coherence. Subordinate well." These last two words functioned also as a release, a "Fare well," so students started shifting and detaching from the circled desks. Mandy stayed behind, fumbling with her laptop and backpack. When the others had gone, she approached Digger's desk, which in this classroom was off to the side, in a corner, rather than positioned normally in front of the board (the projector screen rolled tightly above).

"I added that Danny sentence, it was mine," she admitted. "I had heard about the Goths and wanted to see what other people might add."

"That was not a bad idea," said Digger, but was it true?

"Nobody knew him in my group," she said, "but I talked to him a couple times." Then she added, "I saw on my phone that you were with him on the bridge, Professor Diggerson. Did you actually see him, you know, jump?"

Digger just nodded. He didn't want to talk about Danny and the Bridge, not to a student, especially. Prickling with unease, Digger noticed that Mandy also seemed uncomfortable, her words hesitant, her tan fading. *What was this student's motivation?*

"Everybody knows," she said, and Digger wondered if "everyone" included his own peers, none of whom had said anything about the newspaper report that late morning. Granted, he had seen only Jess Williams, the Humanities secretary, along with a couple teachers in passing, such as Tobias Mann, who once again had not even said hello, just nodded. He was a nodder.

"I heard that those Goths picked on Danny," the girl continued, "so I added that adverb clause to our sentence. I don't really believe it, though. How could anyone talk another person into killing themselves?"

Digger had no answer, even after he had asked himself that same question so often, so he said eventually, "It doesn't seem likely."

He felt flushed, even a little suspicious (*of what?*), and decided to open the room's door, started moving toward it. Then a pair of noon 101 students entered the room, and the air came back in with them. "Hello, hello," said Digger, and the boy and girl greeted him. The girl seemed to know Mandy, who said something to her and then made her way to the door. Before exiting, the student leader turned back to her teacher and said, "I'm sorry about Danny, Professor Diggerson, and that you experienced it. That must have been awful." Then she turned and walked away, not waiting for any confirmation. Digger thanked her retreating back. As he erased the three sentences from the board, he said hello to the newcomers again, wondering if they were wondering about him, picturing him up on that bridge with Danny Jones. He thought of the Goths. The student grapevine (aka the Internet) knew not only that Digger was the unnamed OVC professor, but also that "they" existed, a fact that had kept Digger tossing for hours in the moonlight all week, a fact not mentioned in the Sunday paper and not yet released by the Rockwell reporter from the *Ocean View Weekly*.

Chapter Six: Cause-Effect

More common than its twin focused on consequences (effects), a cause-effect plan built around "reasons" works for nearly all subjects, such as literature (reasons why a protagonist changes), art (why an artist uses a particular color), history (why an event occurred), business (why a particular solution works best), psychology (why someone did something), and on and on. Note that while all topic sentences display a cause-effect relationship with their thesis, an actual cause-effect plan centers on a body paragraph itself, on its structural foundation. A paragraph unplanned usually offers broad, confusing content comprehendible to only the writer, not the audience.

Five days after Digger's conversation with the reporter Jonathan Rockwell, everyone knew about "they," not just Mandy and her unnamed associates (why did Digger think of that word?). Before the week was out, Digger had tired of discussing who *they* could be, and he began thinking less of *them*, too. Instead of fleshing out the villains, conversation tended to dilute their shapes and faces, turning the culprits into the ghosts that Digger now expected them to be. Danny Jones was gone. *Story over*. By a late-October Friday, one that leaned far closer to winter's embrace than to summer's memory, the sad boy's memorial was to take place at 4 p.m. Parking his truck prior to class, Digger had decided definitely to go, but he wondered about his peers, causing "they" to again flicker through his mind. Would Paul go? Although Danny had been his student, Digger could not see his odd colleague developing a connection with the boy, with any student. In his seven years at OVC, Digger had not seen Paul Smith being friendly with anyone, really, except maybe Bill Jacobs, the two guffawing at times, sneer smiling, probably over some student's awkwardly phrased sentence. Back when Bill still liked him, Digger's bitter, bearded peer had presented him with a student's sentence from early in the semester: "Sometimes I take my parents for granite." Digger had immediately known that the student meant "granted," and he had chuckled the way Bill had expected, just not so deeply. "That's a Spell-check mistake," Digger had said, and Bill Jacobs had responded, "That's a classic, one for the wall." Then Bill had copied the sentence onto an index card and pinned it up in the Adjunct Faculty Office. Digger had hoped that the student would never come to see his teacher and realized that such a visit was unlikely anyway.

Shifting his thoughts from the bearded sneer, Digger landed on Gwena Schmidt, the Grammar Nazi. She almost *had to* go to the memorial. As the Humanities Chair, Gwena was just about an administrator, and they would all go, flashing sorrow and concern. *Who was that one with the really round head?* Digger couldn't remember and didn't think that any other composition colleagues would attend Danny's memorial. Maybe Tobias Mann, angling for Gwena's job after next semester. Maybe Don Domberg, who might have known Danny from Tutorial Services. Maybe Joan, the LD specialist, or as she liked to be called "Doctor Powers." *An appropriate name!* Danny had, in fact, appeared to be learning disabled to Digger (due mainly to his reticence and to homonym spelling errors in his papers, such as "there" when he meant "their"), so perhaps the boy had crossed paths with Powers, who scared Digger a little bit. Probably other teachers from other fields would go. *What had been Danny's major?* Digger didn't know, but since the boy had been a sophomore, he had encountered fifteen professors by this third semester. Digger hoped that all fifteen, even Paul, would attend the afternoon gathering.

After leaving his little white truck and this string of musings, Digger soon had to cross one teacher off his list because Paul Smith was lurching up the sidewalk toward the parking lot and a two-door sedan that had once sported bright blue paint. Now, almost white patches blossomed on the car's trunk and passenger side door. Although Digger couldn't see the driver, it must be Paul's wife—Diana? Donna? Paul was angling toward the vehicle. Clean shaven and tall, but starting to stoop a bit, pushed down by time or maybe attitude, Paul Smith reminded Digger of a stork, a villainous bird from a Disney film. Digger imagined that Paul could easily scare children.

The stork had seen Digger, and the two men stopped alongside the blue car. Digger bent and looked in, saw a woman who looked small and wispy (*what kind of bird would she be?* None came to mind), said "hello," and straightened up to Paul. His beak was shut firmly.

"Don't you have a wood-paneled station wagon?" Digger asked, adding good naturedly, "a museum car from the eighties."

"It runs like a tank," answered the stooper, a little defensively, "and will still be running strong long after your little import dies."

Digger doubted that and had learned not to rise to Paul Smith's taunts.

"I love your station wagon," he said. "It reminds me of my childhood. My father had a car just like that." Then Digger remembered that his father had died in a similar car, but luckily Paul did not pick up on this thought. The odd man would have wielded it against Digger.

"My wagon just needs a tire patched. Debra dropped me off this morning." *Ah, Debra.* Paul did not say hello to his wife and did not introduce her, so Digger bent down again to the silent, wispy woman (he could imagine her thin grayish hair moving about, like a small, aging Medusa, or perhaps like lost earthworms on a concrete sea), who had leaned over and rolled down the side window.

"I'm Matt Diggerson," he said. "I've known Paul since I got here." Debra Smith might have nodded or just experienced a tremor, and the little woman sort of smiled, her mouth opening a bit anyway. "Most people, including Paul, call me Digger."

She didn't, saying instead, "You were the one on the bridge." It sounded a little like an accusation. She had sort of a squeaky voice.

"That was me," said Digger, and then nobody said anything. Digger half straightened, poised between the two strange people.

Digger finally announced, bending again to include Debra, "I've been thinking about what the boy said, that 'they' had wanted him dead, and I've been thinking of social media. Have either of you ever written emails that you wished you hadn't?"

Debra started to say something, but Paul spoke over her. "I use email as infrequently as possible. If a student has a question, that's what office hours are for."

Digger wanted to say that email had killed office hours, but then Debra leaned over and pushed open the door, a signal to depart. Digger decided that as a cartoon character, Debra Smith would have been a gray mouse. *Villain or victim?* Digger wasn't sure. He straightened up and moved aside a bit for the husband.

"Are you coming back for Danny Jones' memorial?" Digger had used the boy's full name because he didn't know if Paul addressed students by their first or last names (probably not at all, probably just pointed). Digger used first names, which just felt natural.

Paul Smith seemed to be processing Digger's question, grinding it away in his beak, finding its taste to be unappetizing. Then the tall man said, "Why would I? I didn't know him."

"Ah, well," Digger stuttered, wanting to tell the bird man that after over a month of classes he should have known him, at least enough to mourn Danny's passing, but what good would that do? Digger decided to give his peer an out: "He was hard to get to know. I knew Danny from tutoring last semester, so I'm going. But my class gets out right then, too, so the time's right."

"Not for me," replied the bent man, who then folded himself into the little car, reminding Digger for an instant of a circus, of clowns. Once settled, Paul turned to Digger and said, "Once I leave this place, I don't come back until I have to." Debra Smith seemed to know that her husband had signaled their exit, so off they went—putt, putt.

"Very nice to meet you," Digger said aloud to himself. In his mind, he renamed the pair the Morbids: Paul and Debra Morbid. Mental play often kept Digger from arguing with people, most of whom seemed to like to express their views as facts, and word play blocked out Danny and the Bridge, too.

After the Morbids putted off, Digger categorized them as *them's*, as *they's*, and that unavoidably brought him back to Danny's last words. But had Danny ever met Paul's wife? Could a pair of sad, aging, child-less adults influence a young man enough to kill himself? Who could be so affected by as non-credible a teacher as Paul Smith? Could a student actually admire the negative man, believe him, follow him? *Implausible.* No college professor would have that pull. Perhaps parents, siblings, friends, peers pretending to be friends—teens were so peer-oriented, so gullible when it came to fitting in. Digger realized that he should focus his "they" thoughts on students—if he gave any credence to those haunting musings at all.

As he walked, though, he went back to the Smiths, an incongruous pair: Paul, the metal bird, Debra, the mouse, all air and wisps of hair. Neither would be the hero in any tale other than their own. What about him and Anna? With her long, straight, light hair, her colorful eyes—blue on sunny days, green under the clouds—Anna could certainly star on the silver screen. Digger had noticed how she drew men's eyes, even women's! Women certainly liked to check each other out. Some people said that Anna and Digger looked like siblings, the same coloring no doubt, but Digger knew that he had married above himself aesthetically. Anna could have married royalty, could have travelled the world, ridden through the ocean surf on a white horse (maybe a unicorn), thrown rose petals and benevolent air kisses to the serfs (with him in the crowd, in the mud). However, Anna had chosen him.

But would she keep him? The question startled Digger, and he tucked his little fall jacket around himself more tightly against the cold, autumn's invitation to winter. The cool late-October air swept the walkways of not only earthworms, but other humans, so Digger reached the Faculty Offices Building without having to open his mouth again.

On the third floor, passing by the Adjunct Office, Digger noticed Bill Jacobs, who was usually gone already by the time Digger arrived on campus. With his wooly brown beard, thick enough to store a pencil and maybe even a small notebook, this colleague reminded Digger of an 1849 gold prospector. Quick to speak, fast and steadfast with judgment, Bill Jacobs in a Disney flick would be no animal, just a bearded human with a oversized shotgun. Seeing him in the office, Digger almost walked on past because his former adjunct peer had been mad at him for two years, angry to be bypassed by Digger for the in-house full-time position. In fact, from a distance, across a piece of campus, Bill would not wave to Digger, but instead pretend not to have seen him, just continue on his straight, sure path, plowing through life, beard and attitude first. With blinders like those, maybe Bill wasn't pretending.

Glancing at his watch, Digger stood in the open doorway and said, "Hi, Bill. Long time no see. How's it going?"

"Better for me than you, apparently," said the other, and Digger had to process this greeting before he understood it—*the paper*. "You're the unnamed OVC professor," continued the bearded man. "The newspaper didn't say why you were on the bridge." Bill Jacobs tended not to ask questions, no doubt implying that he already had all the answers, but Digger heard one anyway. Hard not to with Bill's loud and clear voice. With this man, Digger never had to say "What?"

With other colleagues and even with some students, Digger had downplayed his role on the bridge, and he did so again now. With Bill, a person had to have shields raised, protection against an assault of words. For fencing, Digger laughed once and said, "Pizza. Pineapple and cheese from Mario's. It's worth a trip across the bridge on a Saturday night."

Bill smiled, and Digger remembered the look from a couple years ago: the grin of a predator before a walled-in prey.

"Students jump off that bridge all the time," Bill declared, surprising Digger. "The administration's policy is to not publicize the suicides or the attempts. They say that doing so could give other students the idea, as though the looming presence of the Bay Bridge doesn't do that already. They just want to save their asses!"

They? Digger thought about teachers, then administrators, then students, pictured the latter in a line leading up the bridge. Then he asked, "How often? I never hear of jumpers."

Bill didn't seem to know, but he came up with a fact anyway: "Every year. Mostly teens. The second leading cause of teen deaths is suicide."

Digger suddenly remembered talks like this with Bill Jacobs, who always seemed to be full of facts, some of them iffy.

"What's the first cause?" Digger said, and they both pondered that.

Then Bill cast his predator's smile and said, "Probably English Composition."

Despite the subject, Digger had to laugh because Bill's response was so unexpected. It reminded him of when Gwena visited the Adjunct Office a few years ago and told both Digger and Bill about a poll she had found on the Internet. Supposedly, college-bound teens had been asked to rank their fears, and both "parents' death" and "terrorist attack" had trailed "English Composition" in anxiety. Thinking of 9/11, Digger had always found that poll hard to believe.

"Bill," he said, "I'd like to talk with you about Danny's suicide some time, but I have to go to class now. Are you going to the memorial later today?"

"No," responded Bill. "I didn't know him, and I'm not out to impress anyone with my compassion. [*Like Digger was?*] The administrators will make a big show of this not being Caucasian View College, but I'm not interested in their games."

Digger remembered that Bill was big on conspiracies, which of course had prevented *him* from being hired full time.

"Caucasian View," smiled Digger. "You might be right."

"We just lost a quarter of our African-American students," joked Bill Jacobs, but Digger didn't laugh, just nodded, said, "I have a black student in my last class, a hard worker," and moved off to his own quiet office. He had forgotten to ask Bill about email, about regretting messages sent. Bill had probably sent some hot words to Gwena on occasion, maybe when he, Digger, had gotten the full-time position. Digger decided that even mature adults could leave an electronic trail of stupidity.

The afternoon classes plodded by, probably because Digger had something extra to do afterwards, partly because his English 101 students were now analyzing rhetorical elements, which required them to extend their thoughts further than they were used to doing (*tough on their developing brains!*). For his two English 102 classes, Digger had changed Aristotle's rhetorical triangle (ethos, logos, pathos) to ideas that reflected a fictional analysis, so ethos related to the narrator's characteristics and antagonists (not to the author), logos reflected the literary work's themes (not the non-fictional argument), and pathos still dealt with the audience (with the readers' evoked emotions). Heady stuff, this sort of analysis took a lot of practice.

In his last class, the 3 p.m. 102, Digger had watched the black-clothed Goth student—his name was, in fact, Josh, not John—to see if he looked guilty, to fit him into a "they" category, but so far he had failed. Certainly, Josh wasn't the hardest working writer, but he put forth an acceptable amount of effort and had done well so far. He was probably a "better" student than Danny Jones had been—more sociable and open. And Josh was even friendly with Digger's only African-American student, Dennis, who was one of the class' better writers.

After class, Dennis had stayed behind and spoken with his teacher. Dennis had a big smile that formed easily; it was infectious. Grinning, the young fellow announced, "I like that rhetorical triangle. My 101 teacher didn't tell us about that." Then the black boy dropped the smile and switched to his real topic, Danny: "Are you going to Danny's memorial? Danny was my friend, but he was hard to reach. Everybody called him 'Dow,' you know? You know the Dow Jones Index? Well, Danny and I were business majors, and with his name, Jones, the nickname really fit. Danny was up and down, just like the market. He seemed to like 'Dow.'"

Digger said that he would remember Danny as *Dow* from then on and that he was definitely going to the memorial, that they had better get going, too. He thought that Dennis would walk over with him, but the student scooted away too fast after saying good-bye.

Digger walked to the library alone. There, he found about a hundred people, maybe more, a lot of suits and a surprising number of young black people, at least a couple dozen. Digger had not known that OVC had that many African-American students, and he was glad, glad to see them, too. A dozen lines of chairs faced the library, along with a single microphone. The round-headed administrator (*his name?*) was tapping the microphone and making it chirp. Digger recognized a dozen people or so, but only one whom he knew well (fairly well), Gwena Schmidt, the current chairperson.

In greeting, the Grammar Nazi said, "You would think Omar Johns would know how to use a microphone," and Digger registered the administrator's name amid another electronic screech. The sound reminded him of the gulls that swooped and cried above the campus on the sea.

He affixed the name to the administrator's round head, memorizing it. "I'm glad you're here," he said to his chairperson. Then he added, "How well did you know Danny?"

"Fairly well; he was my student, you know. We talked a bit, but I never really got through to him, obviously, since he failed my course."

Omar Johns said "Hello" then, the voice magnified and sounding odd at first, causing a couple of gulls to veer off and complain. "Thank you for coming," he said in a more controlled volume, keeping his round head a bit further from the mic. "We are here today to remember one of our own ..." Digger zoned out. He was tired after four classes in five hours, a schedule that he nonetheless enjoyed and requested each semester, partly because it gave him Tuesdays and Thursdays off (or at least free of classes, if not of office hours and advisees).

Gwena leaned into Digger's slumbers and said, "Omar's pretending to tear down fences, but he's really putting them up. All around OVC."

This seemed like a strange statement, made Digger think immediately of Frost and people's faulty knowledge of the poem "Mending Wall." Then Digger thought *Ah!* and travelled back two years, to his first fall after being raised from the adjunct ranks. Placed on this new level, he and Anna had been invited to the chair's house for dinner, his first and only such invitation (although he had to admit that he and Anna had hosted no parties, either). They had met Gwena's husband, Richard Schmidt, a stock broker. Digger had at first been a little intimidated by the man, partly because the composition professor knew nothing of stocks and bonds beyond the mandatory retirement fund taken from his by-weekly checks. Digger assumed that he would live forever and have the money to do so. About finances, he was not wise.

Standing with Gwena and only half listening to Omar Johns, Digger remembered that dinner conversation, which had gone something like this:

Richard (to Digger): "What are you writing these days?"

Digger (to Richard and then to Gwena): "I'm writing an article about a new lesson I call Positive Peer Review. Should I ask colleagues to read it?"

Gwena: "You can ask me, perhaps Don. Some of the others might get jealous. Sometimes it's better to select your audience carefully."

Richard: "Good fences make good neighbors."

Anna: "Frost?"

Digger (to Anna and then everyone): "It is from Frost. 'Mending Wall.' But everybody gets his point wrong."

Gwena (to Richard, good-naturedly): "Now you've done it!"

Richard: "Done what?"

Digger (to all): "In the Frost poem, the narrator, the speaker, feels just the opposite. He doesn't want to 'mend' walls. He wants to tear down the walls that people put up around themselves. It's the other character, a neighbor, who says 'Good fences make good neighbors.' Frost is lamenting that fact."

Richard: "I stand corrected."

Gwena: "He's a new full-time professor. You have to expect to be schooled."

Digger (just a bit defensive): "I'm not lecturing. I just think that it's interesting that everyone—not just you, Richard—knows that poem, or at least that expression, and that ninety-nine out of a hundred people get it wrong."

Anna: "I think good fences do make good neighbors."

Digger (laughing): "Me, too!"

Then they had all four talked spiritedly about fences, the different types: physical walls, attitudes, distances, finances, cell phones. Digger had offered one of his favorite quotations, from dramatist Harold Pinter: "We use words to hide from each other." Then they had all talked about words and the hidden emotions, such as fear, guilt, shame, even happiness.

Digger had said, "I sometimes hide my happiness with Anna when I'm talking with unmarried colleagues or divorced ones." Anna had mentioned her best friend, Carrie, and her and Matt's somewhat sudden divorce. The conversation had drifted to divorce then and gotten a little gossipy. During some of those tales of peers' woes, Digger had indeed used words to hide some shiny emotions, mainly contentment and pride, a mix at times mistaken for arrogance. On the way home from that dinner, Anna had laid her head against his shoulder as he drove his little white Toyota pick-up, which he loved like a person, especially enjoying shifting the gears in a world gone automatic.

Omar Johns was still talking. He certainly had a lot of words about a fellow human he had probably never met, but maybe Digger was being unkind. He felt a bit bothered. Was it that no other colleagues had invited him and Anna to dinner? *Anna!* Although she had said that she would *try* to come to the memorial, Anna was nowhere to be seen.

Johns was talking about Danny's funeral, which would take place out of state in the near future, and Digger realized that the burial was being delayed so that the family could have an actual body to inter. Gwena leaned in again and whispered, "No body." Digger nodded. He did not plan to attend the actual funeral, probably. Maybe he and Anna would make a road trip, probably not.

With Johns' words ambling on, Digger noticed another known face, Don Domberg's prominently bearded one, heading in his and Gwena's direction. Don's face reminded Digger of an old train's cattle guard, his stiff, full beard brushing humanity to either side as he approached. Digger liked Don; had known him for all seven years at OVC (known him about as well as he knew any of his peers), but couldn't help feeling a bit judgmental about that face full of hair, that shovel, which Digger imagined to be an attempt to stave off middle age in some show of virility. *Why not, though?*

Don stopped crashing through the crowd and stood alongside Digger and the Grammar Nazi, nodding to both. "Nice turnout," he half whispered to them, looking around, swinging that hairy mask side to side. Only a strong wind would shift *that thing*, thought Digger, who realized that the beard made Don appear to be Muslim. That was fine with Matt Diggerson. OVC had a trickle of Middle-Eastern students, who all seemed to be business majors and whom he often used to help at Tutorial Services. Digger had discovered that most of the Saudis and Afghans planned to return to their native countries to take over their fathers' businesses. *A nice deal!*

Gwena lowered her head and asked Don's beard if he had known Danny Jones.

"Just in passing," the stiff beard's owner replied. "He came in for tutoring, worked with Digger a bit, right?" The beard swung over in Digger's direction. The hairs looked course and clean—no crumbs—yet Digger stepped back a bit anyway. He decided that he didn't much care for chin hair, but maybe that was due to the scrub brush that spotted his own face when Digger took a few days off from shaving, a smattering that reminded him of his woebegone backyard bushes. Don Domberg's house-framing shrubbery no doubt flourished thickly. Don was still sort of whispering. "He worked with Joan, I think, but maybe that was another black boy."

That sounded a bit racist, a quality that Digger had never ascribed to Don, who seemed too positive and optimistic to hide shadows such as bigotry. *Who knows, though?* Digger had almost never witnessed racism on campus, just a sarcastic bias against rich teenagers attending college (from certain comp instructors!). Racial bias wasn't something a teacher would bandy about, though, and Digger pictured his colleagues, their faces, which came up white with each cell in the reel. Very few of these faces appeared in the current crowd.

If Danny Jones had seen Joan Powers, then he was learning disabled, for she was the LD authority on campus and had an office off of Tutorial Services. Digger scanned the crowd, didn't see the little battleship, the S.S. Powers (as some had nicknamed her) anywhere.

"I didn't realize that Danny was LD," Digger said to both Gwena and Don, quietly, though, because he didn't want any others to hear.

"Must have been," said Don, who had forgotten to whisper.

Digger turned to him. "I just saw Danny recently, Don," and when the bearded man's eyebrows rose, Digger thought of the newspaper article and added, "I don't mean on the bridge. Before that. I stopped to talk to him on campus."

"Did he say anything?" asked Don, adding "on the bridge, I mean—up there?" Don suddenly didn't look like his buoyant self. Maybe he was showing some empathy for what Digger had gone through.

"He said that someone, that 'they,' wanted him to jump."

"How extraordinary!" exclaimed the bearded man, a bit loudly, so that Digger noticed a couple people turn and stare. Don was too focused on Digger to notice them. "And you believed him, Digger?"

How could Digger answer that question, one that he had asked himself a thousand times? How could he *know*? On this issue, Digger felt as bipolar as October.

"Yes," he said simply.

Silent for longer than usual, Gwena leaned in and said, "You do, Digger? You think that Danny was coerced into jumping off the bridge?"

Digger looked straight ahead, noticing that Omar Johns was still talking and moving his arms about. The composition teacher shook his head up and down a few times, said, "I do. At least today, this minute. Later, I will be sure that nobody assisted in his suicide. I go back and forth, back and forth."

The two other professors seemed to ponder this fuzzy see-saw, and then Gwena said, "You should talk to someone about your experience on that bridge, Digger. Maybe a grief counselor, at least Anna." Digger noticed that the Grammar Nazi's sharp features had contracted, softened, and he appreciated her concern.

"We talk," he said, nodding, knowing that he was lying somewhat.

"Talk to a shrink, Digger, my friend," announced Don, and with a nod of his great brown beard, the head of Tutorial Services swung off, moving successfully through the crowd, shedding people to right and left, carving a path toward the evening. Digger and Gwena watched him go.

Then Gwena said, "Don does not always seem endowed with great empathy."

"Maybe he hides it in his beard," said Digger quietly, and Gwena laughed.

"Could be that."

They stood and listened to Johns. Administrators certainly had a lot of words in their heads, many more than composition teachers.

Apparently tired of Johns, Gwena whispered again: "Ninety percent of suicide victims have mental problems. Maybe Omar should mention that."

Digger nodded again, finding this dark humor a bit too shadowy, focusing on the large number instead, on the 90. *Mental problems.* Maybe Danny had heard voices. Maybe "they" were simply conjured phantoms. Then he thought again of the dark hoods that he had seen (*imagined?*) vacating the bridge that starry, stormy night. Maybe "they" were demons.

Chapter Seven: Compare-Contrast

> *This paragraphing plan works especially well for generating ideas, too, since it stresses a view of opposites, which can create interesting and enlightening juxtapositions, such as positive/negative, optimistic/pessimistic, valid/illogical, etc. In terms of a body paragraph, a compare-contrast block of information can comprise similar elements, contrasting ones, or both. However, quite often, two opposing angles offer the most effective use of this structure.*

In early December, a light snow graced the grounds of Ocean View College, but later that day, the winds would drive the darks clouds inland and clear the path for a spring-like sunny afternoon. *New England!* Digger loved the place. By far, October and May were the region's most bipolar months (as Anna had said), each bookended on one side by cold rains, the other warm sunshine, but all of the other months carried weather surprises, as well. In the Sunday paper, Digger had read about Danny Jones' funeral from the preceding day. The boy's body had never been recovered; his casket held only air, as did the images and memories of loved ones standing or crouched above the grave, their heads lowered to the ground. His mother (only 34—*Why were reporters so age conscious? Just like his own mother.*) was quoted as saying, "He was never any trouble," and Digger thought, *But he had them. Danny had lots of troubles. Now what or who were they, if anyone?*

The article summarized past information, never once labeling Danny's death as "suspicious," just as a suicide, and mentioning Digger's name again. Seeing it made Digger wish that he had gone to the funeral and said something nice about Danny. What could he have said? Admittedly, OVC administrators had emailed everyone about the funeral—time, date, and place—but nobody Digger knew had planned to attend. Anna didn't want to go. "That's a long drive," she had said. She had told him that she missed the memorial at OVC because work had tired her out and she had taken a nap. Digger had thought then of a book to write: *What I Missed While Asleep*. He often thought of book titles, even started stories on occasion, full of energy and hope, but he finished none, just ran out of plot and then enthusiasm. Dreams, he had discovered, could "dry up" as Langston Hughes once wrote. At the end of the *New England Times* article, Digger had been surprised to see the byline "Jonathan Rockwell." Apparently, the reporter had jumped his little ship to ride the ocean-going daily. Rockwell had not contacted Digger after that first call.

"Ch-ch-ch-changes," Digger had sung to himself on Sunday, his mind turning, of course, to David Bowie. Had the rock star passed on? Digger had heard nothing about one of his favorite childhood singers for years.

Drugs often killed rock stars, but who or what had pushed Danny up that railing and off it? What voice had whispered and hammered, "Jump, jump, jump, jump"? The Goth in his late class, Josh the Goth (if he were a Goth? *And what exactly was a Goth?* Was it a religion? Pagan?), had acted no differently than other students. He was juxtaposed only by his attire, leather not being common amongst the OVC student body—the color black, either. Ocean View students tended to be white and well off since minority pupils often could not afford a private-university tuition. For that reason, Bill Jacobs had repeatedly called OVC "Caucasian View College," even though the "C" didn't fit the "O" beginning. Maybe Bill could have said "Oppression View," but Digger did not feel negative about his school, which to him was usually a very positive place. Almost to a head, Digger liked his students, found them hard working enough but not overly grade conscious, easygoing and friendly. A handful of years past, as a part-timer, Digger had thought OVC students to be too apathetic, so to stir them up, he had written "2495" on the board and asked what that number meant. After some silence, one guy had said (seemingly serious), "That's when Star Trek took place." The rest of the class had laughed as Digger shook his head "no." Then another male student had volunteered, "That's when our essay's due," and Digger had laughed loudly with all the eighteen-year-olds. Then he had sobered them up (a bit) by telling them that 2495 was the number of dollars that they (their parents) were paying for a three-credit course. The students had not acted overly impressed by Digger's mathematical trickery, which had failed to churn the apathy much, either. That dollar number must be much higher today, thought Digger, but he no longer knew.

Walking toward his office after his Sunday ruminations, Digger saw both of his old peers—Bill Jacobs and Paul Smith—in the Adjunct Faculty Office. They were both often gone by this late point in the morning—before Digger had even started—but here *they* were, no doubt blasting away at someone. Although Digger had noticed that full-timers avoided the part-timers' group office, he still visited fairly often, liked to say hello at least. "Hi, Bill, Paul," he said as the two strange men looked up at him in silence, as though he were a stranger.

"We're talking about Tobias," said Bill finally, a little leer opening in the brown beard.

"About inviting him to dinner?" said Digger, an attempt at levity, which never got far with these two.

"About him becoming the next Chair," groaned Bill. "The power-hungry bastard!"

"I'll quit," declared Paul dramatically, his own wispy hair fluttering about a bit, and Digger thought of the mousy Debra, of Medusa's snakes, of worms wriggling. Rarely, had Digger heard a more empty threat.

"Why do you think Tobias will be the next Chair?" he asked, looking from one man to the other, although he had come to the same conclusion—*anyone but him*, really, since Digger shied away from that much responsibility.

"I just said why," said Bill, always a little obnoxious, a little judgmental. "Power. Some people just have to have power. Tobias tells *me* about students withdrawing from my classes and how bad that is for the college, implying that *I'm* the one who loses them, not him, and that *I* need to do something. He's lucky to have ten left by this point in the semester. People with power always want to push around those without it. Like us."

Digger wondered on which side Bill put him, but didn't ask. His peer's focus on "power" had reignited those winds on the bridge, and he wondered yet again who would want a boy to die. Was it power that "they" desired? Digger thought of Bill and Paul, who both thought of themselves as not having power but who both acted as though they had gobs of it. Paul had been Danny's teacher.

To them both, Digger said, "Don't worry about Tobias. Even if he is the next Chair, you can both basically ignore him."

"Unless he cuts our classes," broke in Paul.

"He wouldn't do that," answered Digger. "Every Chair knows how important part-timers are."

"Like pawns on a chess board," said Bill, but Digger didn't respond to that. He wanted to ask Paul about Danny Jones.

He turned to the skeletal man. "Paul, you had Danny Jones in class. Do you remember anyone picking on him, anything at all like that?"

"Still sleuthing over the fallen student," said Bill.

Paul laughed, but Digger wasn't sure about what, either Digger's statement about the importance of adjuncts or Bill's about "pawns" or "sleuthing." Then Paul said to both Digger and Bill, "I remember reading off his name the first day of class, you know, to take attendance, to find out which of them was skipping already. And when I called out 'Danny Jones,' this black boy said, 'Here' or mumbled something like that. I was expecting a red-headed freckled Irishman, not a black student. I was surprised to see a black student, too."

Digger ignored this anecdote. To the Morbid man, he asked, "Did he have friends? Was he part of a group?"

"Who can tell? Why are you asking? Feeling guilty?" Paul smiled, and Digger thought of a cartoon crocodile. It would smile like that.

"You two read the paper, right? I mean, you still subscribe to a newspaper? You heard what Danny said to me on that bridge. That's hard to forget? The boy said that *they* wanted him dead. Can you think of anyone he might have meant?"

Their silence provided Digger's answer. He wondered about Paul, Danny's teacher, even about Gwena, his former teacher—one who had failed Danny and another who probably would have.

Then Bill said, "Tobias," laughed, and added, "I blame everything on him."

Paul had scoffed and agreed, but then he added, "What about those weirdoes who are always in the smoking areas? They look like vampires. I had one in my writing class. A girl who never opened her mouth. She looked like she might have contracted something. They all look like they're guilty of something, out there smoking all the time."

"The Goth kids?" said Digger, and he imagined the smoking areas outside various classrooms, attractive white gazebos that the school had set up to keep the few smoking students and staff away from entranceways.

"Sounds like a bad band," said Bill Jacobs, and two of the three men laughed again.

Digger smiled but didn't laugh. Laughter was hard these days, had to be pried open. He remembered his question about nasty emails and asked Bill if he had ever sent any.

"A few choice words to Bob Redlen when he was Chair. The Grammar Nazi has been spared. Gwena has been good to me."

Then the two strange men gave Nazi salutes in honor of the current chair, and shaking his head, Digger left them to their own small powers.

Alone later that day on the third floor of the Faculty Offices Building, Digger looked out his own office's narrow window (the Adjunct Faculty Office had no window), winced at the sunlight, and wished that the snow had continued and that this office hour were over. Across the quad, the library and its twin towers grabbed attention. Usually, Digger thought about kicking a football between the towers, but not today. Thinking back to what Paul and Bill had said that morning, to what his student Mandy had *added on* to her group's sentence weeks ago, Digger clicked on the Firefox icon and accessed Google. *Goths, goth culture* ... Digger typed in the words, hit "enter," and then clicked on the first link, which often seemed to lead to Wikipedia. The Goths had wanted Danny to die: That's what Paul Smith had implied and what Mandy had actually asserted last month. Since then, Digger had thought about doing some research, but something had always popped up, often just simple fatigue, anxiety involving Anna. Since the bridge, Digger had seen Anna less and less, the cats more and more. Shyla and Skittles were the main flames in Digger's current shadow life, and in the soft snow that morning, the two little felines had looked especially cute as they ate on the porch, undisturbed by the flakes landing on their backs. Since Anna had already been long gone to work, Digger had smiled at the cats alone.

On this campus, *alone* must also be how the Goths felt, thought Digger, and then he realized that group solitude, being different, was no doubt the main attraction. Why did people join any group but to be a part of something but apart from something else? To be an 'us,' not a 'they,' but didn't the word depend on the angle of vision? Goths, Digger read from his computer screen, viewed the world from a western white perspective, as Digger had expected, already connecting the term to Germany in some hazy way. But if Wikipedia could be trusted (about as well as the entire Internet), then Goths predated black-clad Nazis, going back to a time when the Roman Empire was crumbling, partly due to pagan tribes like the Goths (Digger saw the term Visigoths, too). Info concerning gothic beliefs contrasted between Christianity on one side, witches and vampires on the other, and when Digger read the word "Satanism," he decided that Hell somewhat linked the two other extremes. Then Digger read some descriptions that fit OVC's little tribe of Hellions: black clothes, dark hair (dyed black), ghost skin, metal accessories. That pretty much differentiated the gaggle of five or so who had passed Digger and followed Danny a month ago. Before knowing one of them, Josh from his 3:00 class, Digger had seen the crows congregating in campus smoking areas, which had always conjured up bird cages in his mind. From behind the bars, the smoking Goths had seemed to sneer at the passing non-pallid—or less pallid (Digger was pretty pallid himself)—world and dare it to sneer back.

Were these Goths white supremacists? OVC's little crow crew definitely looked like Caucasians who chose the moon for their bathing, yet Digger had seen Josh working well with Dennis in his late class. That fact didn't fit, but then Digger thought of Harold Pinter again, of words used to conceal. Could these incongruous OVC Goths actually drive a black boy to his death? Again, that possibility seemed impossible, yet Digger decided to keep an open mind—and open eyes.

He glanced out his narrow office window again, eyes drawn to the library. The twin shadows from the library's towers now began to stretch across the open sunny quad, and for a moment Digger imagined Sauron (from Tolkien), an evil presence reaching out, slowly, surely, to envelope an unsuspecting ivory-tower community. Could OVC conceal such evil? Hopes, dreams, and plans could, of course, turn ugly, and final exams brought buckets of worry. At times, such as this in the fall and perhaps late April in the spring, adjunct faculty anxiety over course offerings could almost sizzle in the air. While Digger no longer felt that prickle, he still saw it in Paul, Bill, the other part-timers. One less class made a huge difference in their lives. Money was often the cause of evil, but it had not factored into Danny's suicide, *had it?*

Digger realized that he should talk all this over with Anna, yet when he was home in the cottage, Digger thought less of Danny and the Bridge, who visited him now mainly deep in the night when sleep lowered his defenses. At home, Digger focused mostly on Anna and the cats, which at present seemed to be mainly what the couple shared. *A phase*, Digger vowed, and those could be endured.

The sound of a mop banging about interrupted his thoughts, which landed on "Richard." Soon the maintenance man appeared in the doorway, and both men greeted each other, Richard's keeping his mop and feet moving, though. Digger had met Richard only after the teacher's morning schedule had changed because the maintenance crews worked after normal hours. After Richard finished the hallway and returned in his sights, Digger called to him, and the short, friendly, elderly man stopped, holding his mop with both arms as though it were keeping him propped up. Probably it was, Digger realized, casting a ray of empathy the old man's way.

"Richard," said Digger, "have you ever noticed … [*What?* Digger suddenly wasn't sure how to ask?] Uh, have you ever seen students being mean to each other?"

"You mean like fighting?"

"More like berating each other, like a group taunting an individual, being mean, that sort of thing."

"You're thinking of that black boy," said the maintenance man. "Everybody knows that you were with him."

Digger admitted that he was.

"These OVC students," said the elderly fellow, half smiling, half frowning, "they're too well off and happy, in general. I've never seen any yelling—except in play—or fighting, and the only ones by themselves tend to be on skateboards."

"Yeah," said Digger, who had seen these sole skateboarders often. "OVC students do seem like a friendly bunch."

"Of course," said the maintenance man, "they don't really notice me at all."

"That's because we're old," said Digger although he wasn't, really, and didn't feel old at all. He just wanted to make the elderly man feel more connected. "Young people notice only themselves."

The old man chuckled, agreed, and then left Digger by himself. The composition professor heard the slither and clunk of the mop begin again and then fade down the hall. Silence fell on the Faculty Offices Building and smothered the empty corridors. The quiet crept into Digger's brain, and the solitary man noticed the coming twilight outside his narrow window. *Didn't silence follow the night, just as thunder trails the flash of lightning?* Not this soundless vacuum, which seemed to be drawing the darkness down with it, not hiding within its folds.

Indeed, it was getting late, *time to go*, office hour ended, another productive turn of the clock's little hand with no visiting students. Email had definitely killed off office hours, but traditions took decades and even centuries to die. Digger envisioned countless empty office hours stretched into the future, all mandated in his faculty contract. This one had expired, anyway, so the composition teacher locked his door, exited the building, and started the long, straight (almost) journey to the faculty/staff parking lot.

Despite a band or two of students, along with some single stragglers, moving across the middle path to the Student Union (to dinner in the cafeteria), the campus appeared almost deserted—typical of a late-Friday afternoon. Psych building silent, Admin locked and dark, but then a door creaked open—a quick rip in the air—and Digger jerked his head to the left to see Doctor Joan Powers ejecting herself from Tutorial Services, housed in the basement of the Administration Building. As she strode up the steps toward him, the doctor's eyes landed and locked on Digger, who tried to smile but found that his face failed to respond. Powers did have power, Digger had to admit. Despite her short stature, Joan had presence.

"Hi, Joan," he said, slowing his walk.

"Diggerson," she nodded, falling into place with him and then increasing their pace.

For a woman who clung tightly to titles, signing her mass emails as "Doctor Powers," the LD specialist was a bit stingy in handing them out herself. Remembering that he had wanted to talk to her about Danny, Digger said, politely, "Are you going my way? I wanted to talk to you."

Powers was short, both height and hair style, probably in her mid- to late-thirties but seemed older. By choice, it seemed to Digger.

"I'm going this way, anyway," she said, appearing unwilling to cede the path to a colleague, but Digger let that judgment flow away.

"You know I was on the bridge a month ago with the boy who jumped, right? [Doctor P kept her head straight but deigned to nod it—once.] Danny Jones, I wondered if he were one of yours, if he had a learning disability." Digger let the implied question hang between them. Thinking of what Don Domberg had said at Danny's campus memorial, he waited, interested.

"He was not registered with me," Joan Powers responded, still striding along (Digger thought of his young self trailing his mother), and he realized that he soon would run out of pavement and that he was also slightly dejected by her response, which seemed to close a mental avenue. "But that means nothing," she snapped, and Digger wondered (not for the first time), "What's wrong with this human!" He waited for an explanation, knew it was built up beneath her strong point, a lake of oil beneath the flame. Joan had her hair so tightly compressed in a bun that Digger feared to stand behind the woman, thought that the barrettes or scrunchies might explode with the pressure, and that little image entertained him as he waited.

"Many LD students go undiagnosed," the young old woman finally decreed, stressing the last syllable of the last word to soak it in judgment. "Even today, when so much more is known about learning disabilities, so many students remain undiagnosed. The number of LD students is extremely high [a number that did not include the speaker, *of course*], so that Jones boy could very well have been LD, but he did not register with me."

"When I tutored last semester, I saw him a couple of times. Did you?"

"No. I didn't know the boy."

Don Domberg must have had it wrong then; the student he had seen with Joan must have, in fact, been "another black boy," as Don had said. He shifted the head of Tutorial Services out of his mind and turned back to the Learning Disability expert.

"Let me ask you this. You know what Danny told me on the bridge, right? You read it in the paper or heard about it?"

"I read that he mentioned someone's wanting him to jump."

"Exactly," said Digger, getting to the crux of his desire to go through an encounter with this prickly woman. "That's what focuses me about that night, about a possible, well, killer, an assisted suicider."

"A Kevorkian." Powers looked up at Digger, and was she actually smirking?

"Between a Kevorkian and a killer, I suppose," he concluded, thinking, *That's close to KKK,* but adding instead, "Is it possible? Could a group of peers persuade a young person to commit suicide?"

The little woman turned back to the walkway, to the future stretched out straightly before her. Digger had noticed that her eyes showed a lot of pupil, big black circles, but maybe that was just twilight's coming.

"Experiments on monkeys," she began (and from the side Digger saw little white lights flash within the dark orbs), "have proven the power of persuasion in primates. Chimpanzees from one group were shown to be antagonistic, mean, even violent, to those from another, and the violence was communicated from one member to another, from peer to peer. In other words, one individual persuaded another to treat other chimps badly. And, of course, chimpanzees hunt and kill other primates, baboons for instance."

Digger had not known about chimps eating baboons, didn't want the image in his mind. The two talking humans had reached the parking lot, and Joan Powers looked out over the vehicles. Digger had an irrational feeling that the doctor was scanning for monkeys. "People are monkeys," she said, and Digger laughed because irrational thoughts and logical conclusions sometimes crossed lines.

"At least *were* monkeys," he responded, still smiling.

"Yes," concluded the doctor, who then surprised Digger by asking about his weekend plans.

"Papers," said Digger. "The last batches before finals."

"I'm glad I'm not a writing professor," the LD specialist announced before breaking off from him and striding away. Digger watched and thought, *So are your students,* but he said instead, "Thanks for the talk, Joan."

Then he stood still for a moment, as though waiting for a bus. He couldn't picture where he had parked, but then he did and went to the waiting little Toyota truck. Seeing it, he wondered suddenly why Danny had chosen the bridge. Wouldn't carbon monoxide in a vehicle have been easier? *Willy Loman's plan.* A long tube to an even longer sleep. Then Digger remembered news events about teenagers who texted *friends* to kill themselves with their parents' cars, with handguns hidden in closets, with pills, teens who urged peers to jump off cliffs, to make nooses, to drink themselves into catatonia. Had any of these bullies ever been prosecuted, punished, jailed? Digger couldn't remember what had happened to those dark taunters. *Involuntary Manslaughter?* What did that mean? Even if he discovered bodies that fit the murky "they," would justice ever be served for Danny Jones?

The cottage was cold. Anna was out, probably with Carrie. Digger remembered past Friday nights that Anna had shared just with him, but now all he had were two feral cats, neither of whom would get within five feet of him. Well, Shyla did wink into his eyes, Digger acknowledged, and he went back to the kitchen to look for his furry friends. They did not disappoint him. *Those cats could certainly pack away the food!* On the top step now, the two rested with tucked in feet, like a pair of black-and-white shoes. When he nudged the back door open, holding a half-filled bowl in each hand, each retreated just a bit, and then advanced quickly on their dinners. Digger watched them empty the bowls, lick their paws, and disappear into the backyard dusk.

An hour later, after darkness had fallen and taken hold, Anna returned to find Digger watching the news. She brought home a pineapple pizza and salad, obscuring Digger's little resentments for a while, but then Anna wanted to go to bed early. "I'm beat," she said, and, "I don't want to watch TV," and, "I have work to do tomorrow."

Digger chose to focus on the TV point because he did want to vedge out before the tube and because they used to do so together. "We can watch PBS," he argued. "You can tell me about work, about Carrie." *And I can tell you about mean monkeys and people*, he thought, but his partner in life had decided to pick and choose, too.

"PBS, I don't want to think that much. I'm too tired to think."

Resentment bubbled up from Digger's dark river: "You're always too tired these days." While he knew immediately that this weakness was a mistake, the emotion felt pleasing in a masochistic way.

"So what if I am! You're always working, too. That's all we do is work."

Digger recognized the truth in these words but failed to see a clear pathway past them. "I just don't want to be alone yet, tonight," he said, not facing his wife.

"You won't be," she responded. "I'll be right in this room, asleep, and you will have better company with PBS."

This room, Digger thought. She means the other room, with a door between them, a fence, and then he remembered, "good fences make good neighbors."

"Good fences make good spouses," he said, but Anna didn't want to discuss that.

"I'm too tired to figure that out, Matt," she concluded, turning from him and disappearing (*like the cats?*) into the bedroom.

Digger went back to the news. Only half processing that the west was burning with wild fires (as usual), that the mid-south was churning with tornadoes (as usual), and that Washington was coagulating, not functioning due to the ideological divide between Republicans and Democrats (as usual), Digger heard Anna exit the bedroom and close the bathroom door, and then reverse that process. She did not bid Digger a "good" night, and he did not have one.

Chapter Eight: Classification

Anything can be classified, any noun, any action even. You just take the topic and break it into its parts. In fact, this organizational pattern represents the key to organized, communicable writing—i.e., taking a topic and dividing it into its more specific sections, which could then often be classified, too, narrowing topics and creating specific ones to then choose and build paragraphs. Without such breakdowns, an essay would flounder around broad ideas that could head in any direction, any confusing path. Thus, classification not only assists in controlling ideas (turning a few into a paragraph), but also provides narrowed topics in the first place, the key to a successful generation of ideas.

They had made a list—the most undesirables—and checked it more than twice, classifying the especially naughty, the not nice. Santa Claus was not real, but he was definitely white. Peers, teachers, others—the list was thorough, comprehensive. They circled one name. Six of the group's members—two had begged off, saying that they would not risk a criminal record—would teach that name a lesson this night. The little group had chosen eight symbolically, the eighth letter of course (A, B, C, D, E, F, G, and H), "Heil" and all that, but they didn't know much about Nazis. Although each had grandparents whose friends had died in the waters off Normandy, the jungles of Guadalcanal, the frozen mud of the Rhine, these very young adults considered World War II to be ancient history, right along with the Romans and just about everything else that teachers wasted their (the students') time lecturing about. They knew all about 88, though (i.e., HH, Heil Hitler), having Googled it, picked and chosen morsels from history's old carcass. Online, too, they had found the address for the circled name: 111 Cottage Road. Sounded quaint. *A good place to break things!*

For the task, they were well-armed: black ski masks (eight black ones from Walmart, just $5.99 each if you could stomach the clientele), black spray paint (after all, his house might be white), and a truncheon for all (who can find a battery when you need it!), each made from a cheap black Walmart sock filled with change and whatever. Just in case anyone needed a good knock on the noggin. Maybe a guard dog. That was the basic message to all on the list. *Watch your friggin' noggins!* Better yet, *shut 'em!*

Omar Johns had made it on the list, sort of, due to his hosting the *black's memorial*. None of the eight had known Johns' name, so they had just written "Round headed Jew administrator." They had added the "Jew" part for emphasis and for fun (many on the list had the word stamped after their actual names). But Omar Johns' "name" was not circled, not yet, and the one that was didn't have "Jew" after it since *Diggerson* didn't sound Jewish, *did it?* The writing professor looked sort of German, but the traitor acted like a "nigger-loving Jew," they decided. Again, history was not one of this group's mental strengths.

The List (they thought of it with a capital "L") revealed a few adults and all of OVC's minority students known to the eight members, a dozen students at most, since these eight came in contact with "darkies" by proxy only, that is, when teachers would use the listed students' names in class. The undesirable

peers looked like this: Hector, Anita, Leslie, Michael
Jew, Amy Jew, Josh, Jennifer Jew, Migel (Magoul?),
Deandra, Amy Jew, Wannita, Dennis. Although "Amy
Jew" was listed twice, they didn't care, for the more
names, the more important the list. Unbeknownst to the
eight, their list was a drop in OVC's bucket of minority
students, many of whom commuted to school. It was a
start, though.

Their plan was to circle a name, one at a time, and
teach its wearer a stern lesson, one that would haunt the
person and put the campus on edge. "Prof Diggerson"
was the first circled for a variety of reasons, mainly
because he was named in the paper and seemed to care
about "the dead darkie," had been asking questions
about the suicide. Also, the group's leader had found
Diggerson's address online, and none of them had
doubted that it was up-to-date. They all trusted the Web
and its gospel truth. Vexing, though, that two members
(*past members?*) had chickened out—the old "got to
study, dude." Maybe their excuse was believable (to
most students, all excuses were believable).

The leader's dark Volvo (at OVC, students often
drove better cars than teachers) would fit six just barely
anyway, not eight, so the non-chickens piled in, making
a lot of unnecessary complaining noises. *What a crew!*

"Take the mask off, moron!" said the Driver to one
of the males in back.

"You're a moron!" said the passenger, but he took
off the ski mask and held it in his lap. Two girls rode in
front, both scrunched into the passenger's bucket seat.
All three in the back seat were boys, young men.

The moron said, "Room for one of you ladies back
here!" whereupon the *ladies* rolled their eyes. One
responded, "Put your mask on, dork."

"You're a dork!" came the backseat voice. The
moron had learned little but pathos from his English

101 study of rhetoric, and probably he had brought those emotional *skills* with him all through childhood up to the present.

As they drove through the early evening's fresh darkness, the driving leader said, "Got your truncheons?" and each of the five other heads answered affirmatively: Yes, yup, yeah, got it, and "truncheon!" The moron had spoken last because he was still defensive about being labeled a "moron," a word that the eight ascribed often to non-group members, and he had repeated "truncheon" because he liked the word. They all did. It sounded unique, solid, and threatening—just as they envisioned themselves.

As the Volvo purred from one streetlight's cone of illumination to the next, passersby would have noticed two rows of three white noses protruding from shadowed eye sockets. Inside the car, the six late teens bantered on, using words to mask their feelings just as they would soon use actual masks to hide their identities. Only the leader, the Driver, felt actual happiness, or perhaps just adrenaline, the rush and expansion of power, his prime motivation, which existed in smaller and smaller amounts behind one pointy nose to the next. All together, the back row fellows—all three brains and hormonal systems—didn't match the leader's surge of ego. In back, fear sat amidst a silver lining of excitement, of rule bending—*their* rules. These three, along with one front-row female, jabbered the most, most of their utterances involving Digger and his African-American (not their words) loving and know-it-all ways.

From in front, the controlled girl summed up the others' conversation: "If Doctor D wants to know what happened to Dow Jones, then he can first find out what happens to curious cats."

This comment sailed right over four heads, but the Driver, turning to her, smiled. He said, "You mean *Down* Jones. Down, down, down!"

The others liked that, laughed and repeated, "Down," sounding like a barbershop quartet warming up and needing practice.

Jones," said the leader, picking up steam. "Davey Jones' locker. Danny Jones' locker! That's why nobody can find him. He's down in Danny Jones' locker!"

Nobody understood this "locker" epiphany, the moron even picturing his own high school locker and remembering all the trophies, such as pens and candy bars, that he had stolen from losers and stored in it. Then he thought "Down?" and "Davey Jones?" Although he didn't remember Danny's last name, the moron laughed with the others and then announced, "Truncheon!"

This parroted term made the car rock with mirth again. They were all having a fine time. The Driver hung a right and was looking at the rectangular white street signs as he drove toward the bay. Soon, the road ended, continuing perpendicularly in both directions, and he declared, "Ah, hah!" He had seen "Cottage View" up on a pole just past the stop sign.

"One eleven," said the Driver, guessing left and then looking right at each house since he had noticed that the even numbers were on the left. The "right" houses revealed small front yards and short driveways since the sea was so close. After passing a dozen or so dwellings, the Driver slowed at a little gray house with white trim in need of repainting. Seeing the number 111 (one "1" was a little crooked) illuminated by the front door's outside light, he announced, "One eleven" and pulled the Volvo into the darkness between Digger's house and his nearest neighbor. A small dark space since the houses on this street were stacked like sardines.

"I'm surprised a professor can afford this neighborhood," said the other girl, whereupon the curious-cat one spat, "These little shacks! They look like outhouses."

Everybody laughed at the idea of outhouse shacks, decreeing that these were just places to take dumps, which was basically what they were planning to do. The laughter fueled four brains, two already filled by other forces—sharper, darker ones.

"Masks on," ordered the Driver, and five rose into place—then the sixth. The moron had dropped his on the floor and could not find it right away in the darkness covering his feet, reaching to his knees.

"Truncheon," he said, but nobody laughed this time.

"Spray paint?" said the Driver, and five voices repeated the words. "Truncheons?" he said, and five voices echoed it. "Just in case," he whispered, and five voices followed. "Stop repeating me!" he laughed, and everybody laughed but the moron, who had begun to say "Stop…"

One door clicked open quietly, then another, then two more, and all four closed together almost quietly— a muffled clunk/clunk with just a wisp of an echo. The Driver had remembered to switch off the Volvo's interior light, and he congratulated himself on this foresight. "Follow me" broke the tense silence.

Six shapes crept up 111's driveway, keeping to the far shadows until the side of the cottage blocked the outdoor light in front. Six shadows passed a little white Honda hatchback and a little white Toyota pickup. The air puffs coming from half a dozen ski masks mingled and mixed with the breathing bay so that the night was almost completely undisturbed by the intruders. Socks hung like clubs from five left arms and one right one, the only left-handed group member. From five right hands (one left), the main tool waited, ready for action.

The Driver whispered, "Damn it, we forgot to shake the cans," and the five others heard his can emit quick, shocking ratchet sounds, which were loud and sent prickly ripples down their sides. "Shake the f-ing cans," he commanded, so more ball bearings flew about, preparing the paint to spray. When it did, the noise was loud, too, but all six persisted in drawing two long crossed lines, each with perpendicular heads and tails. The vandals all worked quickly, fear and adrenaline propelling them.

The quiet cottage at 111 Cottage Road offered no protest, no sudden lights or exclamations erupting. Suddenly, it was all a little anti-climactic. The Driver straightened up and looked through a dark window, could see nothing. The five other shapes mimicked him, could see nothing either, all of the house's windows framing only the shadowed unknown.

"Okay, we're done for now," whispered the leader. "Let's go." One by one, they retraced their shadowed path and returned to the waiting Volvo. "That was easy," said one, followed by another, who said "Quiet," loudly.

A month earlier, in the leader's dorm room, the six founding members had begun calling themselves the "SS" after learning about the Nazis and admiring their power, their ability to wield fear. And because SS had another meaning to them. To the six departing members and the two who had to study, none of whom could pronounce what the SS really stood for, it represented more simply the "Suicide Squad." Power over others. *Ultimate control!*

Driving back to campus, the SS members were all happy, some exulting with puffed-up importance, most relaxing with released anxiety, all reveling in the accomplishment of taking a stand, making meaning, exerting existence, none recognizing or realizing the only lasting effect that their nocturnal visit would have.

Away down the beach, dashing madly into the security of distance, pursued by the intrusion of humanity and by six hissing mouths, ran Skittles, eyes slit and black and forward facing, not back, not back to her sister and to the love of two people who needed it. Into the deepening night, Skittles ran away.

Digger awoke the next morning a little stiff on the couch, where he had fallen asleep after turning off the TV but deciding not to wake Anna. He heard her in the kitchen and greeted her. Then he said, "Coffee?"

When he was sitting at the table and sipping the hot brew, Anna said, "Skittles didn't show up for breakfast." Still half slumbered, Digger responded stupidly, "Are you sure?" Then he said optimistically, "She'll show up soon."

Anna had her doubts, which began to prickle Digger, made him want to shake her a little until the real Anna—the one who liked life, who liked being with him, having a future with him—fell into place again. Instead, Digger shook off the prickly heat himself by getting up and looking out back. He spotted Shyla crouched at the back gate. Facing away from the house for a change, the more civilized sister seemed to be gazing at the sea (the bay). It was a sad image.

"Maybe Skittles took a walk on the beach," Digger said. "At least, that's what Shyla seems to think." Anna looked pensive.

"How's work?" he said to take her mind off the cat (*if that's where it was*).

"Same old, same old," she lamented.

"I was thinking of your student who hugs trees."

"Tommy," she said, smiling quickly, but it faded.

"You told me that your bosses wanted you to stop that behavior and to stop him from flicking."

"He balances sun specks," Anna cut in, and when Digger didn't respond, she said, "You know, those flecks of dust in sunrays. Tommy can balance those on his fingertip, and he flicks one up into the air and just keeps flicking it."

"What's the problem with that? Why does anyone want to stop him playing with the sun?" Digger liked that image, thought it was poignant, and Anna had not said so much to him in weeks.

"Oh," she responded. "Flicking and tree hugging both get Tommy excited, and sometimes he gets too wound up and starts running around and hollering. He can be hard to calm down then."

For an instant, Digger pictured the autistic boy's gliding into the air, where he became Danny Jones, and then the darkness came, then nothing.

"I forget how you're supposed to stop him," said Digger to keep his own thoughts from the sky. "They want you to do something that you didn't like. You called it 'primitive.'"

"They called it that," said Anna, showing a little heat. "They said that sometimes you have to counter primitive acts—you know, like sun speck flicking and tree hugging—with primitive counter measures. Aversion therapy. Behavior modification." Anna mentioned the terms with disdain, the latter one causing Digger to drift back to Danny, a tangent that happened too easily still, a pathway rimmed with slippery leaves and a sharp, deep descent.

"So what do they want you to do?"

"Use Thumb," said Anna, confusing him.

"Your thumbs?" he said.

"What, like thumbs to the eyes!" Anna scoffed. "That will probably be next, but Thumb is a product, a brown liquid. It comes in a bottle with an eye drop. Mothers get it to stop their kids from sucking their thumbs. That's why it's called Thumb. It's bitter, so you stick it on their tongues and the students forget everything else but the horrible taste. The bitterness redirects them."

"Sounds kind of like abuse," said Digger, frowning.

Anna seemed deflated by her explanation. "Sometimes it's all you can do, though. The kids, and they're not all kids, either, some are big and hard to handle. They can't be allowed to get out of control and hurt each other or us. But love and caring are primitive, too, and I can get Tommy to calm down just with those."

She thought about Tommy, at least that's what Digger assumed. Then Anna said, "Sometimes I want to go up to that bridge myself."

"Don't say that, Anna. I was up there. You don't want that."

"I'm sorry," she said. "I wasn't thinking."

"Let's go look for Skittles," said Digger, changing the subject, not that this lost-cat one was particularly rosy. But a beach walk would put off all those papers waiting in his computer, too.

To avoid scaring Shyla up the beach, Digger fixed her a snack of dry food, and after opening the back door, Anna said, "Shyla, come, Shyla," as though calling a dog. The cat stayed frozen, didn't even glance back or even flinch at the sounds, just kept her vigil with the distant wasteland, and in that instant Digger knew that her sister was gone forever. But that conclusion made no sense. Where would she go? Why would Skittles not come back to her sister, to food, even to them? What could have (could be) prevented her? Digger felt the shadow of a cloud, but none yet dotted the December pale-blue sky. *Haunted by Danny and the Bridge. Infected by loss, fear, pessimism.*

Digger put an arm around Anna, who did flinch a bit (or maybe Digger just imagined it), and when the couple reached the grass, Shyla swiveled her head their way (like an owl), both humans noticing her wild half-lidded vulnerability. Shyla's eyes looked like Skittles' now. As they approached her, she scurried beneath the scrub bushes, and Anna cried, "Here's some food, Shyla." Digger broke off from their path to the gate to glance into the old dog crate that he had found in someone's trash and fixed up for his cats, adding an old pillow and blanket, a sweater or two that he no longer wore, but the crate hid no life. Passing Shyla, he told her that he and Anna would find her sister, and the cringing cat watched him the whole way.

Out on the narrow beach, Digger looked up the bay and then down toward the open Atlantic. "Which way?" said Anna. He had not returned his arm to her shoulders, because walking on the sand was hard, clumsy. In the past, he and Anna had strode this shore hand in hand, but at least they were together this morning, side by side, linked by a cause. Digger thought about Anna's direction question and realized that he and his wife had not taken a single autumn beach walk this year. *What was wrong with them?* He turned this disagreeable thought to the more feral of the two little sisters.

"I would think up the bay," he said. "Going up, Skittles would have more beach to run on and probably more places to hide." As he explained, he turned to look "down," seeing the unkempt beach's abrupt end at a short concrete jetty, which stuck out where Cottage View gradually turned up the bay and reached the mouth of the open silver sea. "I think up the bay," he repeated. "What about you?"

"Up," said Anna, turning from the jetty and facing the narrowing bay. "If she ran from something, she would go up the beach, like you said."

"Ran from what, though?"

"Coyotes," said Anna. "Dogs." He had once talked to her about getting a dog, back before they were married, before he was elevated to full-time status and increased responsibilities. She had been pragmatic about a dog.

"Maybe she got sprayed by a skunk," said Digger.

"We would have smelled it. When a car hits one, you can smell it a mile ahead of the poor little body."

"True," said Digger, thinking of a poor little black-and-white body. "What about a person? Maybe Graham and Donna frightened her."

Those were their closest neighbors, a good-natured couple. Graham was an engineer, if Digger remembered correctly. He and Anna sometimes joked about them, neither knowing exactly why. "Maybe they were taking out the garbage, and Skittles got spooked."

"So much that she wouldn't come back in time for breakfast," wondered Anna, adding, "And Skittles has heard us—you—taking out the garbage. She's more used to humans now."

"She is. She has been getting better." They both recognized Digger's present-tense verbs and wondered about past tense ones.

As the two humans walked up the beach, not quickly but not slowly, they kept their eyes mainly on the shore. Closer to the water, Digger swept the surf occasionally, looking for a small black mass, floating, water-logged, but he didn't mention this to Anna. Occasionally, she called, "Tsk, tsk! Skittles! Tsk, tsk!" Digger didn't say much. The bay's waves hardly rumbled beneath the cloud-less sky, but still the water made little licking noises at the shoreline. Here and there, a gull called mournfully, all at a distance. Digger thought about holding Anna's hand, but like a fourteen-year-old at the movies with a girl, he worried about rejection. *Silly!* The thin beach ended after a dozen or so house lots, anyway, turning into rockier areas as the bay pressed inland. Anna and Digger waited at the sand's end and scanned for Skittles. Somehow turning back meant saying good-bye.

When they returned to their own scrubby back yard, Graham the neighbor was hanging over the old wooden fence that separated each home's driveway. He was saying something that they couldn't hear and motioning toward their house. Usually, Graham was smiling (probably partly why they joked about him), but something had made him frown. Fear struck Digger, who thought of Skittles, dead in the driveway, but Graham was pointing at their windows, saying something about "decorating." Digger looked to the right and saw Shyla at the mouth of the dog crate, alone. Close to their neighbor now, Digger heard Graham say, "I see you've been decorating," and then the composition teacher saw the swastikas. Big and black, each about the size of a hula hoop, the Nazi symbols blazed under the sunny morning and rendered Digger and Anna speechless. The paint had dripped down from five of the six swastikas, the *artists'* having held the cans too close to the wall, and one angular shape was backwards, its perpendicular beginnings and endings pointing counter-clockwise, as though the crossed lines were rolling up the bay after Skittles.

"Oh, my God!" said Anna.

"It *was* the Nazis," said Digger, but nobody—not Anna, not Dave, not even Digger himself—knew what he meant. The evil wheels had made him think of Skittles, of the coincidence in time between their appearance and her disappearance, but then he pictured

Danny Jones on the bridge. The "they," his name in the paper, retaliation, perhaps cat napping. Digger knew then that Danny had been murdered.

"What about your house, Graham? Did they get yours, too?" He knew what his neighbor would say.

"No," said Graham (*a little happily?*). "I looked right away, went around the whole place. Nothing. I looked quickly at some other houses, too. Just yours, Matt."

Retaliation. Digger wondered if the cottage's prior owners had left any gray paint in the garage; he thought he could remember having seen a few cans in the corner. He didn't want to have to paint the whole house, though. If he had to, Digger decided suddenly to change the color to green.

"You should call the cops," said Graham. *Yeah, thanks for the advice.* Graham, the engineer, still looked sort of happy, entertained.

Inside, Digger didn't want to call the cops, so Anna did it. Half an hour later, a cruiser pulled behind Anna's Honda. At the computer doing papers, Digger heard the tires crunching the driveway's gravel and went out the front door to greet the police for the second time in as many months. Anna came out, too, and the two cops and two teachers spent about fifteen minutes looking at the six black swastikas. One of the officers took pictures on his cell phone, the other interviewing the *victims*: Were they home all last night? Had they heard noises? When had they gone to bed? How had they discovered the graffiti? Had anything similar ever happened before? Had they any ideas who could have done it? Did they have trouble with any teens in the neighborhood? Any neighbors? Did they have any black paint in their garage? Were they Jewish?

During this session, Graham popped his head over the fence again, and the questioning cop gave the neighbor a similar treatment, abridged though. After every question, the officer wrote in a medium-sized notebook (*for his report?*), and then the five humans, one separated by a fence, two by uniforms, stood in silence and contemplated the nasty black work.

"No tags," said the photo cop to the questioner, and then the speaker turned to Digger and Anna and said, "We have a catalogue of 'tags,' which graffiti artists use to announce their work."

"This isn't art, though," said Anna.

Nobody disagreed. "Probably just kids, a prank," said the interviewing cop. "Has your doorbell been rung lately?"

"No," said Anna, and Graham said, "No," too.

"I used to do that as a kid," admitted Digger.

Nobody responded to him, though, and then the cops left. Then Graham did, too, after adding, "Hope you have some gray paint." His house was white, same as most of the houses in the neighborhood, in Ocean View as a whole, for that matter.

"What a day so far," said Digger to Anna, standing before the swastikas, beneath the sun. "And I've got a bunch of papers to get to, too."

"I'm going out," said Anna. "Errands," she explained. "What about those?" she motioned to the black Nazi symbols.

"I'll do something," said Digger, whereupon Anna went into the front door, Digger to the garage, which was unlocked—too cluttered and nothing to steal. In one corner, he found three big paint cans, one gray, one white, and one who knows what—could it have been black? *No*, the swastikas had been spray painted, the cans had been brought with the vandals, *the retaliators?* The gray can seemed to have about a quarter of heavily swooshing paint, so Digger shook it over his shoulder, one hand on either end, as though it were a giant margarita. Then he found a brush that wasn't too hard and a flat-head screwdriver to pry open the can. When he took the opened can and brush to the driveway, he saw that Anna had gone already, and in about ten minutes, so had the swastikas. The paint blobs were a bit darker than the rest of the gray, but Digger thought they might dry lighter. Later, he would add another coat so that the Nazi symbols wouldn't leak through.

He spent the rest of the morning and early afternoon working on papers, getting up and stretching, looking out the back window for cats (seeing just one), reheating coffee, thinking about vandals and villains, about Anna, about Skittles.

On Sunday, Digger saw that he had once again made the paper, he and Anna both, but the unknown journalist had made no connection between a boy's suicide and half a dozen black swastikas. Even for Digger, that Saturday-solid connection looked tenuous by Sunday, and by Monday—the beginning of the fall semester's final week of classes—the composition teacher doubted that a band of student Nazi wannabees had driven Danny Jones up and off the Bay Bridge. Maybe it was the weather, sunny, almost balmy, leading to student sun-bathing (aka studying for finals) on the balconies of their dorm rooms. Yet Skittles had not reappeared, and Anna still disappeared too often. At school that Monday, Gwena Schmidt, approaching her final semester as Humanities Chairperson, visited Digger's office before his string of classes, saying "Digger, Digger, what's the story with your swastikas?"

"They weren't exactly mine, Gwena!"

"Why you, though? Do you think that you're being targeted?" Gwena could always get to the core quickly.

"Nothing's happened since, but Anna and I have kept both front and back lights on, that's for sure."

"If it happens again, get one of those lights that blares on when someone passes by it. Those obnoxious lights."

"A motion detector," said Digger. "That's a good idea."

"Swastikas!" The Grammar Nazi shook her head sideways a couple times, her lips clamped, angled down. "When your nickname is the Grammar Nazi, the last thing you want to see is a swastika."

Digger told his chairperson that her point was understandable and that nobody connected her to his vandals. "Your nickname's good natured," he said, "even sort of funny. Spray painted swastikas are not funny."

"How did you get rid of them?" He would hear this question quite often.

"Painted right over them." Then Digger said, "Easy, peasy," something he had never uttered.

"Too bad all of life's problems," said Professor Schmidt, "couldn't be vanquished with white paint." She left Digger with that thought, which made him picture a little cat and a light-haired girl.

In both Monday classes (the two earlier 101's and the two later 102's), Digger focused on punctuation, classifying the marks once again (he tended to repeat information in different ways) as follows:

- Commas separate word groups.
- Semicolons balance two statements.
- Colons introduce info: lists, quotes, reasons.
- Parentheses and brackets set off extra info (esp. asides).
- Dashes also set off info—often stressing an example or explanation.

During the editing process of all four of the semester's main compositional projects, Digger had stressed one or more of these marks, such as during Project Two when he compared semicolons and colons, two marks that tended to confuse students. For Project Four, a reflective piece about their writing that semester, he wanted not only to sum up the marks, but also to have students teach each other.

Inventing a peer-presentation exercise, he gave it the odd name SPLAT, which he broke down and classified on the board for each Monday class:

S = Study your designated mark.

PL = Practice to Learn by taking a hard three-sentence quiz.

A = Apply what you learned to your own P4 essay.

T = Teach your peers by using one quiz question (put on board).

For the "SPL" part, Digger had written eight handouts, four for the more complicated comma (introductory, coordination, independent/dependent, and series), one each for the other marks. Since he had students work in pairs, if a class contained more than sixteen students, he simply switched two or three pairs to trios because time would run out on more than eight presentations. If a class were smaller, he would drop the "series" comma presentation since that rule rarely caused students problems—maybe just that some pupils would put a comma before the first item in the series (not common, though) or after the last, where no pause existed and hence no need for any mark.

In his first class, Mandy was the star as usual, and Digger told her and her quieter crony (Kate), "Good job," as the rest of the class applauded their presentation on semicolons, a mark that students misused "seven out of ten times," Digger had stated in order to set up the paired presentation. Most classes clapped after presentations, usually spontaneously, but sometimes Digger would have to lead the charge. Occasionally, Digger would be the only one clapping, a sad sound, but that was rare. In the sociable Mandy class, nearly all eight presentations went well and earned echoing accolades. Two other girls, Caitlin and Leslie, did well with a tough mark, the dash, which most students never even attempted to use. To introduce the dash pair, Digger told the class (as he did four times that Monday) that when he saw dashes used correctly, he usually saw an "A" writer, a fact that tended to focus the young audience.

In his 3:00 English 102 class, the presentations fumbled along a bit, some of the presenters forgetting key aspects of their marks' rules. For instance, the colon duo—Josh (the Goth who didn't seem to want to conquer anyone) and Austin—mistakenly taught the class to put a colon after "such as."

"Actually," Digger corrected, as softly as possible, "you never need any mark right after 'such as' since no pause occurs there, but if you take out 'such as,' then you can add the colon to end the statement and introduce the following info."

"Exactly," said Josh, as though he had just said the same thing, and everybody laughed, even Digger, happy to see his little Visigoth get some sun.

After the last week of classes played out, the papers poured in, the weather continued to defy the coming holiday season, and a series of incidents darkened all the good spirits. First, more swastikas ("copycats," everyone argued, having blamed Digger's vandalism on neighborhood teenagers) appeared, twice in bathrooms (in pen, not spray paint), once on the rear wall of the Recreation Center (black spray paint again). Next, around campus someone had pasted small posters saying "Export Immigrants," which didn't make much sense to anyone. Finally, a Saudi-Arabian student named Mohammed actually got mugged in the big student parking lot (almost directly beneath the Bay Bridge's beginning, the Ocean View side). He needed more than a dozen stitches in his scalp. "They had masks," he told Campus Security officers and then actual Ocean View ones (since a crime had occurred). "They hit me with socks," he said, at first confusing all the cops, who ended up suspecting that "townies" had invaded the ivory tower with handmade weapons. The Saudi student had lost almost a hundred dollars.

OVC administrators kept the swastikas and posters within the tower's walls, but the mugging received a short paragraph in the daily paper since the police had filed a report. The reporter made no connections between any events and the Cottage View vandalism or Bay Bridge suicide, and Digger thought that at least a possible link should have been investigated. He said this to Anna, but she didn't see his point. In the OVC email system, administrators mass sent solemn emails about the OVC community's not supporting "hate" speech, which they said was not "free." They did not expect the incidents to continue, yet suggested that students and staff keep their eyes open. A debate erupted, begun by Campus Security officers (just a handful of those), who advocated that cameras be installed in various places around campus. However, faculty tended to shake their heads at surveillance (too much like a police state for their, in general, left-leaning liking), and the administration cried cost, determined (they said) not to raise student fees or tuition. On campus, the debate died. At home, Digger kept an eye out for nightly intruders, an ear poised for the sound of Anna's Honda on their stony driveway, and a heart open for the return of a little wild beast.

Chapter Nine: Transitional Tactic

Not all body paragraphs require the clear planning explained in these chapter beginnings. Especially in longer essays and reports, you might add transitional paragraphs, comprising even just a couple of sentences (usually three or four, though). These short, unstructured paragraphs function as shifts in thought within your documents, showing perhaps a move from an explanation of problems to a series of solutions, maybe content focused on reasons transitioning to information about consequences. In this way, the short transitional information operates like a train platform between tracks headed in different directions, giving readers a brief rest and pointing to that new path.

The leader of the five pale students in black took a look at his following and found the sight unsatisfactory. A senior, Josh, had never seen them shrunk so low—down to five measly members. Two had graduated last May, and two had started wearing more colorful clothes and not hanging out with them, both signs that the pair had gone *mainstream*. Only one new member fell out of the freshmen class, and his name was Josh, too.

Old Josh inhaled his cigarette, exhaled into the middle of the gazebo that OVC had set up far from buildings to cage off the undesirables, the smokers. Sometimes the Goths would share the structure with white-clad middle-aged cafeteria-working women, other times with chatty Arab students, all of whom seemed to be from Saudi Arabia. Old Josh once boasted sarcastically that smokers were now the most diverse group in America. He often made funny comments that made sense in a twisted way.

For years, the member-changing group had called itself *The G*, not only for Goths, but for Gang, in general, stressing the individuals' solidarity and uniqueness, their distinct identity amongst all the other affluent OVC white students. The five were doing quite well financially themselves, meaning their parents, but the Goths couldn't be bothered with such comparisons.

"For Christ's sake," said Old Josh to the silent gathering. "Look at us. Five left, and two of us Josh's. We should change our name to The J."

That's what they called Young Josh, the freshmen recruit, to avoid confusing names with Old Josh.

"That sounds good to me," smiled Young Josh (J). "I'm J of the J." He had smoked in high school (who hadn't?), but he partook in cigarettes only upon occasion now, such as cold days—like this one.

"Spare a butt, Josh?" The two Josh's contemplated each other. Then Old Josh flicked a single cigarette up expertly from his packet, and, admiring the maneuver, Young Josh picked it out, leaned forward for a light (from one of the two burning butts), and inhaled the sweet heat. Only one other member was breathing smoke into the cool December air, Liz, who had the whitest face that either Josh had ever seen. While Old Josh (the most dedicated Goth) admired it, the young one thought Liz to be a bit creepy, especially since she rarely said anything. In general, these Goths were a quiet crew, far less yacky than the gaggle of crows that others considered them to be. The Goths just looked loud, took up space due to their gathered blackness. Each of the five had been labeled a non-conformist in high school, two of the members, in fact, having been voted "Least Likely to Conform" in their high school yearbooks, a mark of pride, ironically since being highlighted in those popularity tomes was itself a sign of assimilation.

In high school, Young Josh had been in a similar group, but those pseudo-Goths had all flown in different directions last summer, a couple staying in their hometown to work in restaurants, a couple others traveling to distant colleges (one as far as Florida, an odd place for a non-conformist with black hair and an ultra-white face). One member had even enlisted in the Army, which had separated him from his individuality—first from his body (through a shaved head and wardrobe change), then from his mind (through shared verbal abuse, mainly). Young Josh had not regretted his own choice, for he enjoyed OVC and was doing well. He had discovered especially a talent with the pen (the keyboard). In fact, his writing acumen, along with his father's decision to enroll him in some college-prep classes in high school, had allowed him to "comp" out of English 101, to jump directly into the second required writing class, and he was having no trouble with any of his college workload. This little group, though, The G, gave him a place to go and mellow out since his own two roommates were business majors concerned only with making money and bragging about their family businesses. Even when the three shared an occasional beer, Young Josh couldn't connect with their financial focus, which bored him to tears. He was a college student. What did he care about money? And Young Josh could think of no fate more horrible than graduating into the family business, for his own father was a lawyer. The little J had not lived very long, though, and life so far had erected few obstacles other than social ones, which he had helped to construct himself.

The newest Goth took a drag on the cigarette and, as usual, had to suppress a cough. He was out of practice. "I'm out of here tomorrow," he said. "Right after my history final."

"Me, too," said the more talkative girl of the group, Kate, the quintet's main attraction for Young Josh, who spent a lot of time asking Kate out—in his imagination.

"What class?" he asked her. If Young Josh stayed with the group next year, after the other Josh had graduated, the young one would probably assume a leadership role simply because of his more sociable nature. Of course, the leader didn't really do much in the G.

"Abnormal Psychology," answered Kate, and all five Goths laughed, little barks, flames igniting and fading. They all thought themselves to be abnormal. They took pride in it.

"You should do well in that," said Old Josh, and the fires all glowed again.

"What about you?" said Old Josh to Liz. Her laugh had flared out the quickest.

"What about me?" she said back. Liz was prickly, and Young Josh flat out disliked her. But every group needed a strange member, mainly so that the others could stand taller in their own estimations.

"Finals," Young Josh ventured bravely, for he was a bit frightened of Liz, all five foot one of her, if that.

"What about them?" said Liz, but then she smiled because she enjoyed being prickly.

Young Josh wondered why he hung out with this crew. None of them seemed to like each other that much, and there had to be a more enjoyable cluster. These four were undemanding, though, and simple proximity offered some comfort, even Liz's, especially Kate's.

"I don't have any finals," exhaled the smoking girl to everyone and to nobody, and that's who requested an explanation of this dubious statement. Liz did have a lot of crazy art classes, after all.

Smoke rose and curled up the gazebo's circular roof. The cool December day snailed along, and even the non-smoking Goths could see their own exhalations. The more attractive girl left first, saying, "Stuff to do," and Young Josh thought about stuff to do with Kate and what stuff he had to do without her, too. He had submitted his final writing paper a couple days earlier—just that History test now. It felt good not to move, and he imagined a pride of lions spread out in high grass. Proximity did bring some comfort.

"Bye, Kate," he yelled to the departing black back. Nobody else had bid her farewell.

"It's too bad about that black kid," J said to the remaining G after a bit, and he looked at the three white faces, saw that each had heard what he said and then shifted back to embellish his comment. "You know," he continued, "the guy who jumped," and he nodded his forehead toward the Bay Bridge, which took to the sky at this top end of campus. The three other white faces turned to the monolith, and their gazes and brains stuck. That bridge had a way of grabbing a person's vision. Young Josh followed the invisible line from their eyes, which led him to the top of one of those great shoulders. *Did the black kid climb up there?*

A person passing by might have wondered what had attracted the four strange students, what had drawn their attention and kept it frozen. Young Josh himself wondered what the others were thinking.

"It's hard to imagine what he was thinking," the newest Goth member said, and he could have been talking about anyone.

Out on the back sidewalk, stalking quickly away from the Faculty Offices Building and from another successful bout with office hours (*no students!*), Professor Tobias Mann stared over at the four smokers and wondered what they were looking at. *The bridge?* He was glad they weren't glaring at him, as usual, and he glared at them instead. What were they supposed to be? They looked like delinquents, not college students. In fact, they looked like that old Alice Cooper rock creep, and the Humanities professor had always hated that screechy "music" and ridiculous makeup. What was that old hit? *"School's Out!"* It should be out for those smokers.

Mann kept his legs churning on the straight path to the parking lot, but he kept his eyes on the smokers, too. They were up to something. If Tobias had his way, OVC would expel oddballs like that, yet his classes were increasingly full of them. *Separate the wheat from the chaff. People should go where they belong,* he thought, almost saying it aloud, and he decided to tell his wife (Amy) about this crew. *Over scotch.*

After passing well beyond the gazebo, the middle-aged man shifted his mind to a more pleasant topic and concern, Gwena's leaving and his acceptance of her position as Humanities Chair. He had been at OVC longest now, *except maybe for Robert Redlen.* Redlen had been Chair before, though, *a pompous bastard,* a failure as the Chair. Still, some colleagues didn't seem to warm up to Tobias himself. When was the last time he had been invited to a dinner? Amy's cooking could use a little imagination, but maybe he should do some inviting. Grease the skids, so to speak. He was respected, though, and that's what mattered most. Maybe he should write a little more, this winter break, do something scholarly, create yet another wordy report about some *mumbo-jumbo*. So much of that these days. *Student this and student that!* That Diggerson liked to write, some of it published, too. But Digger was too young to be chairperson. *Not yet, Diggerson! I wouldn't mind raising your wife up, though,* thought the old letch, and Mann smiled as he walked past the Administration Building, which made him think of Don Domberg down in Tutorial Services. *Would that old phony be elected?*

He shook that idea away and began searching for his car, could never remember where he had parked the damn thing. That irritation shifted his mind to adjuncts, whom he did not hold in high esteem. They all wanted his job, and all they ever talked about was teaching, not about the important parts of being full-time, such as the committee work, the guiding of advisees through academia, the publications to review (and occasionally to write). *Oh, yes*, he would make some changes with the adjuncts, cull them out a bit, *the chaff.* Just like those smoking vampires, some adjuncts had to go.

Professor Tobias Mann was a great believer in fences.

From his narrow office window, Matt Diggerson watched Tobias plow up the sidewalk, saw him glance repeatedly at the smokers' gazebo, at the Goths smoking away the late afternoon together, and imagined his colleague's dark thoughts. *Exterminate the crows*, no doubt. Digger recognized Josh among his handful of black-clad friends and realized that the young man was now basically an old student, a piece of the past, for fall classes were now finished. Digger looked back at the long, straight walkway and considered using it himself very soon. In the distance, before being obliterated by leafless trees, Tobias appeared to look over at the pale students again, and Digger searched for the older man's thoughts. Dreams, obstacles, a gratitude for another painless day beneath the sun? Somehow, based on Mann's countenance alone, Digger did not think gratitude to be commonly conscious to the departing professor.

Shadows stretched and died across OVC's quad, and Digger realized that his small office was now dark, that he was sitting alone in the growing night. Outside, one of the Goths had broken from the gaggle, but Josh remained. Digger saw the boy exhale smoke and imagined a series of expanding white rings, rising and vanishing. Josh was innocent, as innocent as any human could be anyway. He had been friends with Dennis, Digger's only African-American student, and Josh had never looked away or acted ashamed at the mention of Danny Jones. Digger realized that Danny, like a smoke ring, was floating out of his thoughts or perhaps burrowing deep within them. Digger's own Anna anxieties were pushing the boy from his mind, quieting the whisper of "they," obscuring the wide eyes and all those stars. At times, though, both worries raced side by side through Digger's mind, usually at night when the rest of the world seemed to be sleeping, gone, and as Digger tossed about near Anna (or increasingly on the living room couch), Danny Jones would pull ahead and dominate his dreams. But these vaporous images blossomed less and less as the Fall semester came to a close.

Classes had ended earlier in the week; Digger would no longer see his English 101 or 102 students, who would march on into their futures. After he graded their final papers (online), would Danny simply slide away, perhaps down in a ripple of guilt to Digger's black river? Soon the year, too, would click ahead to a new number, and the Lost Boy would truly become a part of history, labeled and dated. *Let old acquaintance be forgot* ...

When he glanced out the window again, Digger was unnerved to see the remaining Goths, Josh included, staring at his window, but quickly he realized that they were looking beyond him, could not possibly see him through the narrow window and within the dark office (he had not turned on the light). No, the "crows" were gazing at the sky or maybe the Bay Bridge. Maybe they were discussing Danny.

Present and past, thought Digger, and this moment within this twilight seemed to symbolize an end of sorts—the semester's conclusion, the year's passage. Soon, history would glaze over the past months just as the sea had done to Danny Jones, all those all-important incidents—big, small, and in between—that make humanity's present seem so much more meaningful than past events or future undertakings, all those moments stuck now only to memory, that tenuous grasp.

Sitting in the dark, alone above a gaggle of crows, Digger vowed not to forget Danny Jones, to find justice—if any existed.

Chapter Ten: Process (Stages)

This organizational plan seems self-explanatory: the steps or stages in a "process." For stages, which tend to be broader than steps, often a single body paragraph will cover one level, itself broken down into narrower topics, which could follow any organizational pattern— effects of that stage, opposite sides of it, parts, examples. If a single body paragraph covers more than one stage, then often the writer will be providing an overview of the overall topic.

For Digger, winter break—which began when he submitted his fall grades via computer (usually a week before Christmas) and ended with the start of the spring semester, late in January—was the best time of the year, a stretch of five weeks when he could rest his mind, relax at home, work on his own projects, and plan for the spring (he loved planning): a sweet process he called vacation. This year's winter vacation would not taste so good.

It began, as everything seemed to these days, with the past. "We travel with a corpse in the cargo," Henrik Ibsen once said, and Digger understood the dramatist oh too well. "A corpse?" he would think through his five weeks of peace. "I'm dragging more than one: Danny, Skittles, maybe my marriage, my lost father, my failings, my dreams." Digger had thought that he was living his dream, that life could go on just as it had before a boy flew, that it would progress along its basically smooth, fairly simple path. But Anna had basically stopped talking to him, ceased communicating, anyway, and the ghosts had started. The ghosts of Danny Jones. Were they real? Digger had seen the boy's saucer eyes that night: those depths had seen specters, had heard them howl.

The day after submitting fall grades (the usual 20% A's, 50% B's, 30% C's, give or take a letter), Digger thought about ghosts, Googled "Bayside Police Department" for the phone number, and jotted it down. On the BPD site, he looked for the cop from the bridge, but the wide, friendly face didn't jump out clearly from the dozen postage-sized photos of officers. Since just two women were depicted, Digger thought that he recognized the older one with those sunburst wrinkles around her eyes, but he wanted to talk to the big man from the bridge. From the list, he could not recognize any names either—of cops or titles. Something to do with "Special" (that's what one cop had said that night), yet it couldn't be "Special Police" or "Special Detectives," could it? Deciding that he would wing it, Digger called the general BPD number.

"Bayside Police Department." A female voice.

"Hello," said Digger. "I'm looking for Special … Special Investigators."

"I'm not sure how 'special' they are, but I will connect you with Special Investigations." The voice clicked off before Digger, feeling dumb, could say anything or even laugh, and the phone buzzed in his ear, was picked up in the second mid-buzz.

"Special Investigations." A male voice.

"Hello," said Digger again. "My name is Matt Diggerson. I teach at Ocean View College and was on the Bay Bridge when a student jumped last October. Is this the officer I spoke with that night?" Digger thought that he had summed that up quite well.

"It sure is," said the male voice. "You lost my card?" More of a statement than a question, good natured, though. Digger thought, *What card?*

"You must be a very good investigator," he said instead. "Good assumption making."

"We're all special here," said the male voice. "Actually, Officer Patty Johnson patched you through. If you had my card, you would have reached me directly. The name's Myles. Do you remember now?"

"Definitely," said Digger although "Myles" rang no bells. He wasn't sure if that were the detective's first or last name. He decided it was probably the last.

"What can we do for you, Professor Diggerson?"

Hm, thought Digger at this remembered addition of his title. "He is special!" But he said instead, "I wondered if you discovered who 'they' were. The 'they' that Danny mentioned on the bridge, before he … jumped. I've been, sort of, haunted by what he said."

"*They made me*," said Special Investigator Myles, echoing Danny Jones via Matthew Diggerson, and for just a moment Digger thought that this cop was making fun of him, of Danny, of the suicide. "We could find no 'they,'" continued the policeman, "and we tried, Professor Diggerson, we tried. We interviewed family members, a lot of those. We interviewed friends, not so many of those. We interviewed his teachers, they hardly knew him. We checked his laptop, did you know he had no Facebook page? They all have Facebook pages. Facebook has been a great boon to law enforcement, the information crooks put on their Facebook pages!"

Digger had had little communication with police in his life—a speeding ticket in his teens (that cop had been a bit terrifying), his father's accident (that one had been quiet, efficient, controlled, respectful)—but this Myles guy was much more sociable than Digger had expected, not remembering him much from the night on the bridge. *Sort of wordy*, thought Digger. He must be lonely. Bayside was apparently too boring to be special. Then he wondered quickly who Myles' "they" were: *They all have Facebook* and *a lot of family members*. Was this cop prejudiced? Digger saw bias everywhere these days. He would have to tell Anna all about this cop. She would be interested—probably, maybe. He wasn't sure anymore. Digger pushed that thought away. He said, "Do you mean criminals who video their crimes and put it on YouTube?"

"Oh, we've seen plenty of that, Professor Diggerson. "That and more, but young Danny Jones was a rare breed. No social media. No Facebook, no Instagram, no Twitter, hardly any emails even, and no threatening ones received. Sent or received."

"And what about his cell phone?" All of Digger's students had cells. They were hooked. Images, messages, immediate gratification—the pull of a drug.

"It went down with him," said the investigator. "His mother said that he had a phone, but we never found it. Not at his home, not in his dorm room. He had no car, and if the phone was in one of his pockets, we never found those either. The electronics would have been fried quickly anyway, by the salt water. Of course, we tried very hard to recover the body. Not even the Coast Guard could find it."

Neither man spoke for a few seconds, each thinking of the endless sea (at least Digger did). Then Digger thought of Anna.

"Is that all, Professor Diggerson?" The social cop apparently had to get back to waiting by the phone.

"Yes," said Digger a little reluctantly, but then he added, "Is the investigation over then? Will nobody ever find out what Danny meant, by the 'they,' I mean?"

"When new information comes to light, we will investigate it. If there is something to find, we will find it."

Digger wasn't ready to let go. "Did you hear about my swastikas?"

"We did," said the talking cop. "We keep track of the goings on in neighboring towns since we're all basically one village."

No fences, thought Digger, imagining the spread of crime. *Maybe we should have fences.* "Did you think," said Digger, hesitating, "that my vandals could be connected to Danny's suicide, to the 'they'?"

"Not likely," answered the cop. "Two completely different scenarios, not really comparable."

"Okay," said Digger, but he thought that connecting the incomparable was often the only way to see a situation from a different angle, the only way to objectivity. "Thank you, Officer Myles." Should he have called him Investigator Myles?

Then the man surprised Digger again: "Did you get that help I mentioned on the bridge, Professor? Have you talked with someone about the young man's suicide? Being a witness like that is traumatic. A person needs to let it out."

To let out the trauma.

Digger couldn't remember having received this advice, which he thought was very wise, except from the Grammar Nazi and Don Domberg. He said, "Yes, I have talked about Danny a lot." He wasn't really telling a lie since he had talked with Anna, his mother, Paul Smith, Bill Jacobs, Gwena, other colleagues, too—and even a doctor, a powerful one.

"I'm okay," he said to the strange sociable policeman. "I'll be fine. Thank you."

"All right then," said Special Investigator Myles. "Feel free to call us at any time with any information. Good-bye."

Digger heard a click. He was still holding the phone to his head, so he cradled it. An old Saturday Night Live skit passed through his thoughts. He and Anna and Carrie and Matt used to stay up late on Saturdays, drinking beers or wine, to watch that show. "Isn't that special!" he mimicked to himself, but the connection memory failed to make him smile.

Stage Two of Digger's winter break shifted into the holidays. For Christmas, Digger and Anna always went to his mother's (Jean Diggerson's) house, partly because she lived alone, mainly to avoid going to Anna's mother's place, which required a shorter drive but no safe haven at the hour-long trek's end. Deena was difficult. Nobody was good enough for her Anna, including Matt Diggerson. Holidays made the woman particularly cranky, which made the longer drive to Jean's house much more bearable. In New England, a person could drive across the region (three states across basically no matter where the drive began on either end) in about the time it took to transverse Texas' Panhandle: four hours. During the three-hour trip to his mother's, Anna and Digger listened to the radio, which in the past had been left off. This time, Anna had said, "Let's listen to Christmas carols," and then clicked on the radio and found one quickly, that strange "honkdee-honk" melody about a donkey named Dominic. It made them laugh and filled in the conversation gap a bit. Music provided a balm, even a silly holiday song about a mule. For their reticence, growing gradually into the norm (*a phase!*), Digger didn't blame Anna completely, because he knew that he was preoccupied by Danny's death, by work (more than he realized since becoming full-time), by the creepy vandals, and of course by the absent Skittles, a little wild creature who had wormed her way into his heart and then left a hole.

At the old homestead, it took Jean Diggerson ("I'm sixty-five now, Matthew.") less than a minute to unleash a dam of anxiety. Before her only son— unplanned and unexpected—could even pour a cup of coffee for Anna and for himself, she tossed a grenade into Christmas.

"Your sister is getting a divorce."

"A divorce?" Anna said, letting the word hang, as though to study it from different angles.

"A divorce!" Digger said, scattering Anna's question, as though the word were foreign, unfathomable, something to scrape off a shoe in private.

"A divorce," his mother repeated, unemotionally, as though she had come to terms with its reality. Of course, she hadn't, and throughout the three-day visit, Jean Diggerson fretted about her daughter, who *had* been planned.

"Jim's impossible!" his mother would announce in the midst of other subjects, such as the tastiness of the food. And then soon after, out would come, "And Emma's not far behind!" as though nobody else had said anything between the announcements, such as the soft inner warmth of the rolls or the turkey's crispy skin. Digger would wait for the inevitable concluding remark that, "I'm glad your father did not have to see this!"

So, so often, Digger wished that he had. A dozen years prior, his father, a lawyer (not the type to advertise late at night on TV), had perished in a car accident, a client's ashes buckled into the passenger seat in an urn since Robert Diggerson often did estate work. Digger had always imagined that the dead helped his father to squeeze out of this world and into the other, the shadow land. Since his father's toxicology levels had shown no culprits (Digger had known that they wouldn't), and no black swerve marks had signaled anything sinister, the death was ruled a vehicular accident and filed away. When he visited his mother, though, Digger still saw his father—in paintings that he loved (such as one containing some black-and-white hunting dogs, a startled pheasant), in trees that he had planted, in the settling-with-time stone wall that ringed most of the property. Digger even felt his presence in the shadows of many rooms: "Dad?" *Just his imagination.*

His mother was still very real. Accustomed to her anxiety and to its verbal releases, Digger both cringed under the Emma lament and empathized with his mother's emotions and words because it would be hard to have a child whose life could not support a happy marriage. No grandkids, either. Digger thought of Anna and their current divide and knew it was just a phase. Too much work and other shadows: Danny, Anna's broken children at work, Digger's endless line of advisees, committees, scholarly papers to review (and occasionally to write), student papers to process, lessons to create, vandals to uncover, cats to find, and over all of these the looming presence of the bridge and "they." *They! They?* That must be how his mother felt—all her fears and obstacles slithering and growing, refusing to be set in any order. But Digger internalized his antagonists in order to deal with them, to get some control, rather than his mother's using her mouth to release the hounds.

"You have to let things out," his mother had advised him repeatedly over the years.

"Why?" he had responded when he was old enough to understand life, or at least his small part in it. "When you let a problem out, it just gets bigger, or seems to."

"Oh!" his mother would exclaim. "When you're my age, Matthew, you will understand."

Anna these days definitely leaned toward his way of handling stress. She illustrated it herself, a fact that almost turned Digger into his mother at times. About Emma's pending divorce, Anna volunteered little but always connected her point to Carrie, her best friend (*other than her loving husband, right?*). Anna would say, "Carrie's doing well by herself and so will Emma," and "Carrie told me that the decision to split up was really hard, but that she felt better immediately." *Bully for Carrie*, Digger would think but not say, for his thoughts would turn to the other Matt, the let-go one, the forgotten man, his old friend. Since Anna had wanted to support her friend and since Digger was used to her making their social plans, he had not contacted Matt for a couple years now. The two of them used to watch the Celtics together. With the two most important women in his life making statements that he didn't want to hear, Digger decided to connect with Matt again— maybe after Digger dealt with some of his current troubles. *The phase.*

The ghosts. His mother interspersed her derision for Jim (and less often her daughter) with comments about Digger's brush with death. For three days, Jean Diggerson seemed as obsessed with "they" as her son had been for three months. More than once, the elder had concluded that *they* "must be family," that "only family can affect a person so, good and bad, Matthew, good and bad."

"Why?" Digger had asked, for even though he agreed, he wanted to know his mother's reasoning and to avoid shifting to her reference to "bad."

The sixty-five-year-old woman had surprised him with her shortest explanation ever, a single word: "Roots!"

"Roots?"

"With family, you grow roots, roots that go way back to other generations. Even you and Emma are rooted to your grandparents, even though you never even met them. Even though they passed before you were born, even before Emma was, you're rooted to them through me. Family history, family drama. All the stories, the shared experiences, the bonding. Blood is thick, Matthew!"

Hearing Anna mutter, "Not my family," Digger smiled at his wife and then turned and said to his mother, "But a person can create roots with non-family members. Look at Anna and me."

"Look at Emma and Jim. Family roots are strongest."

"What about work connections?" Digger would not give up this argument, which seemed important. "You can work at a place long enough with others to create roots."

"Have you?" His mother looked pleased with herself, her chin jutted up a bit.

Seven years. Fourteen semesters with the Grammar Nazi, Don Domberg, Bill, Paul, other full- and part-time faculty, with Jess Williams, known librarians (to say hello) and a few technical people happy to help Digger with his Sakai software needs—Digger had rarely seen any of these people outside OVC (a few times at the local supermarket: *Hello, hello*), had been invited to one dinner only (the Schmidt's), had extended no invitations himself, either. These roots were pale and sickly, and he thought of the worms that climbed atop a concrete sea after rainstorms.

"We're rooted to our cats," Digger offered, but then he thought of Skittles, of an empty beach.

Due to circumstances (unseen forces?), to responsibility, to plot, to whatever, Digger realized in those three days at his mother's house that he had far fewer connections than in the past, that he had quit trying to grow roots.

As his winter break progressed into January, Stage Three stretched out and left more bitter crumbs, for at home in the cottage, he and Anna engaged in disagreements, testiness, little fights. The toughest stretch occurred even earlier, between Christmas and New Year's, because both teachers had that time off and because winter arrived in all its finery, snowing them in with each other, with their resentments and secrets. One night, the power went out, and the two people had to sit in darkness and listen to the howling winds. In past winters, they had reveled in these moments, these times when the world shrunk just to them, but now Digger felt as though two worlds were bouncing around the cottage, both with shields raised, weapons locked.

Amazingly, when Anna returned to her special-education teaching a week into January, Digger was glad. Shyla had weathered the storm well. Prior to the blizzard, Digger had covered the old dog crate and wood barrier with a canvas tarp that he found in the garage. Over the tarp, he had piled bricks that the previous owners had once fashioned aesthetically around the now spindly rhododendron and holly bushes. Now, Shyla could just duck under the tarp and enter a warm (less cold, anyway), dry, cozy cave, and she did, staying in the crate most of the time, no longer looking out the gate for her sister, more resigned to the loss, it seemed, than Digger felt. Perhaps the wild teaches you to accept, thought Digger. *Accept or perish.*

With Anna gone, the cottage became a tomb—cold and silent, the type of silence that has fingers, pulsing and probing—yet when she returned, their silence was

154 *Planning to Die*

even worse. It hurt. It dragged Digger's heart down, and he could feel the lack of words and warmth in his throat.

In his gut and esophagus, Digger spent the rest of January with these heavy pains, his mind dully focused on due dates and lesson plans for the spring. Gradually, his enthusiasm for the semester's fresh beginning blossomed, as it always did. A reviser, Digger enjoyed tweaking his assignments and lessons plans. This spring, he had decided to connect his classes' first three papers to a theme: teen suicide.

Chapter Eleven: Illustration

The simplest of plans, an illustration structure comprises a paragraph built on evidence, on examples, on specific proof that becomes the actual organization. In other words, the topic sentence is not broken into steps, stages, reasons, effects, opposites, or any other narrowed topic; instead, you narrow the topic sentence's topic itself and then get right to proving it with a "For example" that you follow with another, and then perhaps another. Often, high school English teachers highlight only this organizational plan, a good one because it stresses specific ideas (the topic sentence) and development (the structural examples). For college papers, though, if you rely just on this simple plan, you will not be thinking critically enough about your paper's topics. Use illustration only when your idea is especially specific and when no other more interesting structural strategy emerges.

Near the end of Digger's winter break and start of the spring semester, the newspaper announced that the Fallen Boy had been diagnosed as a schizophrenic, that the police had found pills for that mental disorder in his dorm room, in a single as he had had problems with roommates in his freshmen year, troubles that had led administrators to house him by himself, a rare but not unheard of situation. Digger read and realized that Special Investigator Myles had lied to him, or not lied so much as left out some truth, since the search of Danny's room had occurred long ago, not recently, so on the phone Myles had already known about the pills, about the schizophrenia (*the voices, no doubt*), perhaps had even come to the conclusion that Danny's "they" were just ghosts, conjured villains, figments of a broken imagination.

Perhaps the talkative cop had even suspected Professor Matthew Diggerson, who looked much more white than black, than Danny Jones, who could have driven the lad to the top of the world and tossed him off. *Heave, ho, my lad! Up and at 'em!* When he was frustrated or a little angry, Digger would let his mind go like this, cast off to hook the deep, those sightless creatures with big jaws. Thinking of the lying policeman, of prejudice, Digger remembered picking up a date at her house one summer during his college years, a Jewish girl (*a JAP*, one of his friends announced to a puzzled young Digger, who had never heard of a Jewish American Princess). When her parents opened the door and saw Digger with his light hair and blue (sometimes green) eyes, they had stood in shocked silence, teaching Digger how prejudice felt, but making him sort of laugh, too. After that date, Digger had made the parents happy by not calling the girl back (*what was her name?*), and since the princess had chosen not to call him either (to transform Digger into a frog), that relationship ended the way many do, not with hurt words, but with apathetic silence.

Everything ends with silence. "We scratch our way into it at conception," Digger surmised, "and slip off into it at the end." Digger pictured his internal black river, the blood-thick flow, and realized that reality— life itself, existence—was its antithesis, a bright sea, the bubbling progression that stretched to the horizon, not the black line that slithered into the past. *Yin and Yang.*

The Asian cultures knew the score. Digger wondered if Danny's voices had been kind at times, not all negative ones beseeching him to drag his worthless self to the top of the world and to fly from it. *They?* The mystery was solved. Voices in Danny's own head had wanted him to die, had planned his path. *But who had put those voices into the boy's head?* Schizophrenia, but had anyone helped?

Throughout January, Digger had felt Anna's ghost when she was out and the cottage's rooms—all fairly small anyway—had begun to contract. In the silence of his living room, with just the sea's winds whispering or at times moaning, Digger had felt Anna's ghost in the kitchen, but when he had entered it, she would have moved to the bedroom. From the kitchen, he would look out at Shyla's crate (he no longer added "Skittles"), perhaps see a corner of the tarp flapping, and wonder if it bothered the little cat and if he should tuck it under a brick (he would). Anna's ghost was sad and lost, not the being of light that had drawn Digger and given his life sure meaning. All January, picturing this spirit and his own corporeal self, Digger had thought of Mary Tyrone, her drug-induced wandering. *Long days, indeed.*

The spring semester's arrival shifted his mind from past to present (*no other choice*), giving Digger purpose, adding steel to his sagging frame, and in all four classes (two again focused on non-fiction, two more on fiction), he decided to begin with a narrative essay, partly because students tended to like creative assignments, mainly so he could focus on their grammatical habits, which were sticky things, obstinate. For instance, nearly all students used too many weak verbs (*is, are, was, were,* etc.), which led often to wordy phrasing, weedy sentences that proved difficult to uproot (*weak verbs and family,* thought Digger).

With a narration, especially, the sentences needed imagistic verbs, so although students would tell few narrated tales in future college essays, Digger saw the advantages to this opening assignment. On his directions sheet, he began with this information:

> Purpose: To tell a story (either fictional or real) that illuminates the problem of teen suicide.
> Audience: The OVC community—perhaps through the *Gull's Call*.

The latter was the name of the school's monthly newspaper. One of these years, Digger expected to be asked (told) to be its faculty advisor since Chairperson Schmidt (Gwena) had asked him about it during his interview for the full-time in-house position a couple years past. In fact, the Grammar Nazi had been part of both of Digger's hiring groups, the part-time one long ago, the recent one, now drifting into the past, too, like everything.

For the narrative's audience, Digger had mentioned the *Gull's Call* because, whenever possible, he liked to make his assignments "real" by offering publication potential. In the past, he had required students to compose feature articles for local papers, letters to their parents, even reports to presidents (the school's or the nation's). One student had even received a form letter in thanks from President Clinton. That had been a good day.

The spring semester's third class brought February with it, along with January's growing blanket of snow, and since Digger's schedule seemed set in stone, he again had four classes on Monday, Wednesday, and Friday, two 101's (11:00 and noon), two 102's (2:00 and 3:00). On Tuesdays and Thursdays, he would be able to do committee work, help his advisees (not much action until April's end, though), process papers, in general keep the plot flowing, and on the other three week days, he would come home very tired. Who cared, though, these days?

Steel, thought Digger repeatedly, and in all four third-day classes, the teacher focused on focusing since even a narrative assignment required planning and clear points so that readers knew why they were perusing the tale. As he entered the day's fourth and final class (a 102), he said hello to Mandy, who seemed to have followed him from 101 (she had earned an A-) to the second required composition class (or maybe she had just been placed there, maybe in secret she despised him! Who knew when it came to the thoughts behind people's foreheads?). On the first day, Mandy had seemed honestly happy to see Digger, who was glad, too, because his lesson plans needed leaders, even ones who could be a little pushy. To teach peers, Mandy offered the necessary student mix of sociability and determination.

The girl smiled, as well, at the big square die (a single dice) in Digger's hand because she had seen it twice the previous semester for an exercise Digger called Focusing For Freedom. Its goal was to illustrate effective topic sentences by leading students to create those TS examples themselves, and for part of their motivation, students could earn free minutes—i.e., early exits! To explain the cube's presence, Digger would write this on the board, usually a white one (requiring ink markers rather than chalk):

1 = Classification—types, elements, etc.
2 = Illustration—examples.
3 = Process—steps, stages.
4 = Cause-Effect—reasons or consequences.

5 = Compare-Contrast—similarities and/or differences.
6 = One Free Minute!

These numbers, of course, related to those from the big die, the size of a softball (white with black numbers), a toy that had travelled with Digger since childhood, one that his students played with now.

In his Mandy class, Digger used the roster to assign numbers (one, two, three, and four) in order to make four groups (the fourth had just three students since one was absent—*a bad sign so early in the semester!*). Then he explained the focusing lesson for the fourth time that day: "For this first narrative essay, not all of your paragraphs will have a clear internal structure, the kind that all your college essays and reports will require, but some will. Look at the Harry Potter books. J.K. Rowling often builds focused, organized paragraphs that classify Harry's choices or that show steps taken, maybe a pair of opposites. For us, for your narrations, you might do the same thing, especially near the end of your stories, where you might build a paragraph of reasons or consequences, as a synthesis for your tale. Remember that planning is thinking, even for this Project One essay. Okay, now the fun part. To earn your freedom, your minutes, you need to help each other to create effective potential topic sentences for your narratives' body paragraphs and to use the five main organizational strategies to plan the TS's possible content. In other words, the TS (topic sentence) can help you to generate ideas for a body paragraph."

Then the composition instructor referred the class to the numbers and corresponding organizational patterns on the board, explaining that whatever number the big die landed on would guide their thinking for a topic sentence. A "great" TS would give the group three free minutes, a "good" one two minutes—with one minute for all four groups if the die rolled a six. Digger offered this great/good judging criteria for their topic sentences: clear, specific, and fit the plan.

Digger held up the die, which was solid but looked like the fluffy ones teenagers who were now grandparents (great grandparents?) used to hang from their rearview mirrors. "Ready?" he said.

"Six, six, six …" chanted Mandy's group, catching on fast.

Digger tossed the die up, not too far because he wanted it to land on his desk, not crash around the floor, and it bounced a couple of times, spun a bit, and then stuck. Looking down at a "2," Digger said, "Illustration. That's the plan your high school teachers stressed, and in 101 you probably built paragraphs around examples of language types, such as connotative words, or some other rhetorical element, maybe metaphors. It's a structure that requires a narrow topic, one that you would immediately prove with examples. It's also the perfect plan for a narration body paragraph or two, so think of your possible stories. Are you telling a fictional tale or perhaps focusing on a troubled peer from your past? What idea would you need to illustrate directly? What idea would be followed immediately by 'For example'?"

That was enough guidance—time to let the students learn by doing and teaching. Digger let the groups work. In general, it took about five minutes for students to get a focusing example on the board, and as they worked, Digger would mull around and answer questions, as long as one wasn't, "Is this good?" For those, he would say, "Ask your peers," or "Put it on the board to see."

He would always remind classes that every example on the board helped—the great, the good, and the not-so-good. All helped everyone to understand why a topic sentence would work or not.

"Remember that the best topic sentences are short," he called out to the working students, "because long ones contain too many nouns, which can confuse readers about the paragraph's actual topic. Let's see some short TS's on the board. Time's rolling along."

In this 3:00 class, all four topic sentences were nice and short, incredibly so. Off the white board, Digger read to himself as follows:

Examples of teen suicide.

Danny Jones was frightened.

The future revealed two paths.

The pressures to end his life was strong.

Of course, the Danny sentence (Mandy's group) grabbed Digger's brain, even more so than the subject-verb agreement mistake in the final example. *Danny!* But wasn't that what he wanted with this paper? Wasn't he trying to help himself and these young people to understand suicide, especially Danny's (beyond the probable cause of schizophrenia), and to do a small part in preventing more? Digger thought of Danny's wide white eyes. *Oh, yes, he had been frightened*, and that detail could be a structural point. *What else?* His voice maybe, his clutching at the railing, his words. Okay, that TS could lead to an Illustration paragraph, actually to any paragraph, though—to reasons, steps, elements to fear. Then Digger shifted to the other three TS examples, the first being an obvious fragment (*but the idea worked*), the third and fourth being good TS's, just not for Illustration as the planning pattern.

Then he explained most of these thoughts to the waiting groups, awarding the second TS (Mandy's group) three minutes and the first one two minutes (one subtracted by the fragment, which made the statement less clear, one of his criteria), suggesting that some research, though not required, could add some strong substance to their stories. He lauded the third and fourth TS ideas, but explained that they failed to "fit" the plan, Illustration. "Look at the plurals," he said, reading "paths" and "pressures." "Those topics are the structures for the paragraphs, multiple paths and pressures, not multiple examples, although each *path* and *pressure* would have to be illustrated, too."

Some students from the third and fourth groups cocked their heads a bit, and Digger laughed to himself, thinking of dogs. He liked dogs. These head cockers would get it in time, with practice. He decided not to label the patterns of these two losing TS's, because one of them (Compare-Contrast or Classification) could be rolled next. He explained this, too. Then he asked the winning Mandy group if anyone wanted to toss the die, and Mandy accepted—without looking at her peers, Digger noticed. She sprang up, took the cube, and pretended to throw the square high and hard, but she was just joking. She tossed the die as Digger had modeled, and it bounced, spun, and landed on a "4" facing up.

"Cause-Effect" yelled Mandy before Digger could make the announcement, and Digger smiled again. Although the well-tanned girl was a little obnoxious, her teacher had to admit that she had learned her stuff last semester.

Digger repeated Mandy's mantra, and because he could not assume that the students' 101 teachers had taught them the names of the organizational plans, he gave another little lecture: "All topic sentences have a cause-effect relationship with their thesis, even with an implied thesis (which your narrative essay should offer, either direct or implied), since all TS's are reasons supporting the thesis, the main point. For a Cause-Effect body paragraph, though, either reasons (causes) or consequences (effects) structure the body paragraph itself. Do you follow me? And don't focus a paragraph on both reasons and consequences, because that would create a big shift and too much info for one paragraph. Choose either causes or effects, just one of those topics."

Students nodded, and Digger wondered if they actually understood so soon since organizational skills took knowledge and practice, both of which this early lesson plan was supplying. *Great if the ideas stuck so soon!*

Soon, though, Digger saw that just one group understood (or perhaps the members had just gotten lucky), for just one of the four topic sentence examples showed a Cause-Effect winner:

> Five thousand teens attempt suicide per day.
> The Goths badgered Danny Jones for various reasons.
> The future revealed two paths.
> Teens often have peer problems.

The Goth statement shocked Digger not because it reignited his "they" obsession, stirring the corpses, but because the TS was so good, and he felt good himself about what he had accomplished with Mandy last semester. His teaching had transferred to other assignments, and that was always his main goal—to teach skills that students would use in future papers.

"This first example really makes you think," Digger said. "Five thousand! That's what, one hundred per state per day? My math skills aren't so strong."

One hundred attempts daily? Maybe in big states like Texas and California, and Digger thought, *Right and left, Republicans and Democrats—neither side brings contentment and peace.* Not mentioning these political thoughts, Digger instead told the class to be suspicious of statistics.

"We Googled it," said a member of the first quartet as though the Internet's omniscience put an end to any manipulations involving their discovered "fact."

"Be suspicious of the Web, too," laughed Digger, but then he said, "Let's look at that fact as a topic sentence. What would the next sentence be?"

Nobody could think of one, but then a guy from the first group said, "For example, New York."

"Nice try," said Digger, "but then your TS would have to be something like, 'Certain states have high amounts of teen suicide each day,' and that would be a division of the 'certain states,' not a Cause-Effect structure. Though interesting, and sad, this five thousand stat is too narrow of an idea to build a body paragraph around. However, two of the next three TS's could. So two groups will earn three minutes each since two TS's would lead to Cause-Effect paragraphs. See which?"

All three groups still in the running for minutes announced that their TS's would work, so Digger explained, "Reasons would structure two of these paragraphs [Mandy cried, "Various reasons!"] while one would break its topic into two parts. Which one?"

This questions was specific enough to give the answer, no doubt because of the reference to "two." Digger smiled at the third quartet and said, "Thought you'd take another shot with this one. It is a great idea, just not for a Cause-Effect paragraph." Even with the disclaimer, four mouths frowned.

To the whole class, Digger said, "I love this 'two paths' idea, which could lead to a great Compare-Contrast paragraph. Opposites. Makes me think of Frost's two paths in a yellow wood. Now look at this second TS, see the prep phrase 'for various reasons'? That's a great way to stress the paragraph's plan to help the reader see the structure, to give the reader a hierarchy to follow. This fourth TS lacks that phrase, but it's still probably Cause-Effect [the fourth group, the one trio, bounced happily] because it would probably be built around the different 'reasons' they have 'problems.' If it were built around the 'problems' themselves, then it would be another structural pattern, so I'll give this TS two minutes."

Then Digger looked at the clock (over the door in this room) and saw that he should get the class moving, but then one member of the trio (Digger didn't yet remember his name) raised his hand. Thinking of his name, coming up blank, Digger gestured to the student with his hand and a nod.

This student was about to take the class on a bit of a tangent, one that Digger couldn't help but follow. "I know Danny Jones," he said. "I mean I knew him, and he wasn't bothered by those Goths. They're harmless. They just wear weird clothes and like to look tough. They had nothing to do with Danny, with his jumping. I heard it was the SS."

Nobody said a thing. Silence reigned? Digger ran the "SS" through his memory banks and could find nothing but Nazis, which led him to six black swastikas that he had painted over, to the administrators' late-fall emails about other vandalism involving those evil images. Finally, he said, "The SS? That's a World War Two term for German Nazis, for Hitler's special troops within the German army. What do you mean by SS?"

"That's it," the boy said, adding one more word: "Nazis."

The word hung in the air, seemed to ring a bit, to echo, but nobody reacted outwardly to it. Digger realized that World War II had no meaning to these young people, that they probably considered Hitler and Genghis Kahn to be contemporaries.

Then Mandy laughed, said, "Nazis," and the spell broke.

Digger wasn't sure how to respond to these events, so he ignored some and said that Danny's "suicide" was a tragedy and then continued with the focusing game. He asked the boy who mentioned Nazis if he wanted to throw the die, and he did. The lesson progressed, and after another winning topic sentence (this time for a paragraph structured around Process—i.e., chronology), Mandy's group earned enough minutes to leave. Digger approached the four students, who were already packing up their laptops into shoulder bags (they had already calculated their earned minutes), and congratulated them on their work. As Mandy exited ahead of the four, Digger heard her say, "Nazis" again and then laugh. He wondered what was so funny about that word. His star student was beginning to bother Digger, who decided that one semester was perhaps enough for both student and teacher.

Ten minutes later, the last two groups (who had earned just six free minutes each) rose to go, so Digger approached the boy who mentioned Nazis and asked him to stay behind. Since Digger's class was paperless—no printed handouts or student papers, all available or submitted online—it took the teacher much longer to learn students' names because he didn't have the opportunity to return papers and connect names to faces. This early in the semester, Digger basically knew nobody, so he said to the somewhat tall fellow, "Your name is …" and waited for the gap to be filled.

"Tim," said the student, who was fidgeting a bit, rocking from one leg to the other and glancing at the door.

"You're not in trouble," laughed Digger. "I just need your help."

"Okay." Digger's words had focused the student, who now met his eyes and waited.

"Tim, did you know that I was with Danny when he jumped, that I was going by on the bridge and tried to stop him?"

Halfway through the question, Tim had started nodding, and now he said, "Oh, sure. Everybody knows. You're famous, Professor Diggerson."

Smiling, Digger said, "Danny, that night, told me that 'they' wanted him to jump. When you mentioned this group of students, the SS, the Nazis, did you mean that they had something to do with Danny's death?"

Tim looked at his feet. "We hear things," he said. "You know, in the dorms, people talk, brag, mouth off."

"Some students bragged about getting Danny to jump?"

"Well, maybe not about getting him to jump, more about getting certain people off campus, getting them to leave, making OVC more—you know—white."

"Racist people?"

"Yeah, some racist people, definitely. Not many, though. I mean, I didn't care that Danny was black. We were both business majors, both in the same dorm, North Seven, and I'd visit Danny. He had his own room. How cool is that! I'm stuck with a couple jocks. Anyway, Danny and I talked about business assignments and professors. Danny had a lot to say, once you got him to say anything. He was my friend."

"But you know students who thought of him as an enemy, just because he was black?"

"Well, I've heard people who don't like black people. You know, you hear all sorts of things in dorms."

"Who did you hear, Tim, one of these SS students?"

At this point, though, Tim seemed to run out of words. He glanced at the door again. Then he said, looking at the wall, "I'm not sure I should accuse anyone."

"Tim, this talk will not go beyond us," promised Digger, who had not thought beyond this conversation, had not grappled with the ethics of knowledge. "It's just that I made a vow to Danny that I would find out who 'they' was, that I would not forget him, but I'm out of clues, Tim. I agree with you about the Goths. I had a Goth student in class last semester, and he was great. He was no villain. I don't know if these SS students are villains or not, but OVC has had a rash of Nazi vandalism lately, so any talk of a student group named the 'SS' needs to be investigated. You see that, right?"

"Okay," said Tim, looking Digger in the eye again. "I know just one name, two guys but one I don't know, the quieter one. He's sort of funny looking, but the loud one's name is Michael." *Michael? That narrowed the suspects down to about 500 students*, thought Digger, since the name was common. Then Tim continued, "He's a little older than I am, a sophomore, I think, a real jerk. I heard him laugh about Danny's suicide. I heard him use the 'N' word." *A sophomore Michael? That narrowed the suspects down to about 150 students.*

"Do you know Michael's last name?"

When Tim didn't respond (the door seemed to have his attention), Digger repeated, "This conversation's just between us, Tim. I won't run off and accuse this

Michael or get him into any trouble that could be linked back to you. I won't tell anyone who told me about Michael. Did you know that my house was vandalized by some Nazi wanabees? I had swastikas spray painted on my house."

Tim was nodding again, and Digger was a little surprised that the boy knew since he imagined students not to care about any events beyond OVC's borders.

"Okay," said the student. "His last name's Kraft, and I wouldn't even have remembered it if Kraft wasn't the last name of the Patriot's owner."

"Robert Kraft," said Digger, thinking of his favorite NFL team, of the benevolent looking owner, his white hair. That Kraft was too old to be a sophomore's father, but *Kraft* was not a common name. "Think they're related?" he asked the boy.

For the first time, Tim laughed. "No," he said, adding, "Michael's always going on about the New York Jets. You know, chanting, 'Jets, Jets, Jets' like they do even though their team stinks every season."

"No wonder Michael's so angry," said Digger, making Tim laugh again.

Chapter Twelve: Process (Steps)

Often, a Process paragraph focuses not on full stages, but on specific steps. For this body paragraph, chronology works better when the process is narrowed—e.g., don't explain your writing process in general, but maybe your editing process or, even narrower, your editing for punctuation steps or, perhaps better, your editing for comma use. At some point, such as editing for one type of comma rule, a writer can narrow too far—true for any planning tactic, but especially for a steps process. If you can't break a topic into narrower ideas, then either illustrate the idea a few times or back up a step and plan again from that slightly broader level.

Leslie Gomez was troubled. She had struggled through the fall semester and managed to do acceptable work, had earned a 2.7 GPA. A commuter, Leslie had responsibilities that few of her OVC peers could even imagine, including unpaid babysitting duties for two little sisters and a part-time job at a convenience store that had been robbed twice (not on her shift) in the last month. Since her mother, technically an illegal alien, had given birth to all three girls on American soil, at least none of the daughters had to worry about their own deportation, but Leslie feared for her mother, who worked long hours on the docks in a fish-processing plant. Her mother smelled like fish. Their home did, too, and Leslie worried constantly that she carried that stench wherever she stood (worried unnecessarily). She was a quiet girl, didn't raise her hand in class, did her work and went home to the fish smell. Last semester, she had liked Professor Diggerson's class because he didn't lecture at them or make them sit around in a large circle talking. They actually did things and sometimes even earned time off for smart behavior, as she thought of Digger's free minutes. This semester, though, class discussions were about all she encountered, and she felt guilty about not participating, yet not confident enough to do so. She felt like an outsider, as though she were not a part of anything, but she was. She was a part of the List.

Sixteen eyes perused the List. They were making progress, one step to the next, a name circled, a deed done, and a circle crossed off—twelve so far, seven this semester alone, an average of almost one per week. "Professor Diggerson" was circled and slashed, along with several student names. Next up, "Leslie."

One of the two girls present said, "She was in my writing class last semester. She's a Spick, a commuter, of course. I followed her once to the parking lot."

The speaker paused then to soak in the eight's admiration for her initiative. Some on the List were impossible to locate this semester, so circling names had gotten harder. Hearing this news about the listed Leslie, though, the leader circled that name and said, "Got cha, Spick!" Then he asked the girl with the initiative what kind of "piece of crap" the commuter had for a car. All mouths cackled at the assumption, which they took automatically for a fact. None had ever driven a piece of crap. They couldn't even conceive of the shame.

"A white Jap car, circa the 1980's," scoffed the girl. "Sort of white. Looked like it had been puked on [more cackling, and one male said, "Puked on!"]. It had a bumper sticker, too."

"Ah!" said the group as one because each member (seven out of eight, anyway) realized that this bumper sticker could be found.

"What did it say?" said the leader. "Something about lesbians!"

"Hug a Fisherman," said the girl sarcastically, as though that were the last action she would ever take.

Hug a Fisherman? That idea was hard to fathom. The SS members laughed and fidgeted, some picturing images of big fishing boats with nets, others of men in streams and on beaches, holding rods and wearing high leather boots. Those were good.

"Slug a Fisherman," said the leader.

"Plug a Fisherman," said another male.

"Mug a Fisherman," said another, and everybody laughed, thinking of the Arab from the campus email, the one who somebody else had gotten to. Full of admiration, the SS had spent considerable time discussing who.

"That's the one," said the leader, adding, "We could've done that!" and then, "But it should say 'Mug a Fisherman's Daughter'."

"Bug a Fisherman!" said another male.

"Shut up, moron," said the leader, and everybody laughed again, this time at the moron.

"You're a moron!"

The girl who saw Leslie's car said, "We can mug her car, break something."

"I know," said the moron (whose nickname was actually Shrek since he had a big head), "Let's poop on it!"

"Poop on you," said the leader, laughter breaking out. "What are we supposed to do, squat on it? That

174 *Planning to Die*

sounds like a job for you, Shrek. First, though, we need to make a statement or two, one step at a time."

Leslie felt flushed with excitement. For the first time in Psych class, she had volunteered her opinion, her knowledge. She had read the chapter, understood the concepts about personality (related to some of it), and thought of a thoughtful response. Plus, none of the others students had known the answer. So she had raised her hand *(oh, how vulnerable that had felt,* her arm up for all to see), and when the teacher nodded at her, she had said, "Introverts aren't always quiet. They just don't mind being alone."

"Exactly," the bearded professor had said, his eyes looking large and a bit wild behind his glasses, and that word had bounced happily about her mind ever since. *Exactly! Exactly!*

When she reached her mother's Civic, the word disappeared, replaced by a deflating sound, for her right front tire was flat. At first, Leslie had no idea what to do, but then she told herself that it was just a flat and wondered how to change it. A male student walked by, noticed the problem, and said sort of stupidly, "Flat?" Then he asked if anyone were coming to fix it? Then he showed Leslie how to do it, the key being to find the needed spare and equipment (under the matting in the trunk) and not to un-tighten and then tighten the lug nuts when the car was jacked up. It all made sense. It was no big deal.

Still, as she drove home, the wacky professor's "exactly" had lost much of its verve and volume. The spare "tire" looked half the size of a normal one, seemed more like a big black donut than a tire, and she worried about it all the way home. *Was the car tilted to the left?*

Her mother told her not to worry, that the tires were old, and one of her uncles was able to fix it. The tire would get older yet. In Spanish, the uncle told Leslie's mother that the tire had no hole, that the air was just let out. Leslie's mother then told her because Leslie's Spanish wasn't fluent, her mother's having decided to raise her daughters just on English. "Who would have let the air out?" Leslie said.

Two days later, she found a note under her windshield wiper: "Mug a Fisherman's Daughter," it read. *Fisherman!* Who knows? Who? Then Leslie remembered the bumper sticker, which another uncle had put on the car as a joke, sort of. She crumpled the note, looked around her, saw nobody, and threw the wadded up paper under an SUV.

Two days later, following the Monday, Wednesday, Friday schedule, Leslie Gomez approached her mother's car with trepidation. From across the lot, she noticed something on the hood, thought that it looked like a potato. As she got closer, the object came more and more into focus. *It can't be!* It was.

Thinking about that lank, the eight laughed and laughed. All anyone had to say was any word related to "feces," and the joy would blossom. From the List, the name "Leslie" now sported a double line through it, a swastika.

"That turned out to be a great idea!" said the leader, congratulating the moron, who beamed. Shrek had few starring moments.

The two girls laughed along with all six young men as they sat around the leader's room, drinking peppermint schnapps. The talkative girl was flushed with alcohol and mirth and camaraderie, the pink bleeding through her winter tan. "I'm just glad you did the squatting, Shrek," she said.

Flushed with his success and acceptance, the moron replied, "Next time, you do it, Mandy."

Digger, of course, had not made the connection between Mandy and Michael Kraft, but doing so turned out to be fairly easy, just a matter of a few steps. The first was to see the Registrar, Joan Leonard, and ask about Kraft. This Joan was just about the polar opposite of the LD specialist, Joan Powers, because this one smiled often and exuded the impression that she existed just to help whoever had requested it.

Because of student confidentiality, though, this Joan looked a little skeptical, so Digger said, "I really just want to see what he looks like." Actually, the composition instructor *really* wanted to see the student's records.

"His picture, I can do," said Joan Leonard, turning to her computer and tapping away at the keyboard. After a series of taps, the Registrar twisted her computer screen to face Digger, standing alongside Joan's desk, and said, "Here's Michael Kraft. Anyone you know? What do you think of him?"

The latter question was a good one. Although he did not *know* the student, he looked familiar nonetheless. He looked rich. What did Digger think of him? He didn't like the face. Maybe because the young man looked right into the camera, showing no embarrassment, no self-doubt. Young people should not be so omniscient. Maybe it was the upward thrust of his chin, a dimple balanced squarely (Digger thought of his own dimple), a defiant pose. Did Kraft also display a slight smile or was that lip curve a sneer? Michael Kraft showed a tanned façade, dark blond hair brushed back in a wave. He looked young and carefree.

"He looks rich," answered Digger finally, and Joan Leonard laughed.

"Most of them do," she responded.

And familiar? Digger knew that he lacked the authority to review the boy's files, so he asked, "Has he gotten into any trouble at OVC?"

Expecting the administrator to deny this request, Digger felt the pull of expectancy when Joan Leonard instead turned the screen back to face her, bent toward it, and then scrolled down. Digger watched Michael Kraft's confident image gradually rise and disappear. Suddenly, with those clear eyes no longer boring into Digger's, the professor remembered where and when he had seen Michael Kraft, the memory bursting into life from last semester: the sidewalk just outside the Admin Building's front door, a warm October day after a rainy night, earthworms, Danny Jones, the Goths, the second group of students, three of them, one Mandy, one a big-headed fellow, the third, this face, Michael Kraft.

The SS member, a wanabee Nazi, was friends with Digger's best student (both last semester's and this one's), and Digger thought not of the young man's arrogant face, but of Mandy's confident one, of Amanda Jenkins.

Chapter Thirteen: Definition

For most college essays, short definitions can be added in parentheses after simple terms (i.e., like this), but occasionally more content—such as a full paragraph or even an entire essay—will be needed for complex definitions. In the case of a paragraph, a classification structure will help you to break a complicated word into its parts, and for an extended definition, those parts can focus their own body paragraphs and lead to Illustration structures, probably, examples of each part. Thus, think of a Definition plan as basically either Classification or Illustration.

Sorrow. Digger knew that everyone had his or her definition, yet they all contained one central word: loss. The loss of a person, a pet, a possession; the loss of trust, of faith; the loss of self—mental, physical, spiritual. What had Danny Jones lost? His life, of course, but what about before the jump, before the pull of eternity? A loss of enthusiasm, of friends, of dreams, of stature, of peace. What about his mother? She had lost birthdays, grandkids, a face looking down with love at the end. Danny's brothers? They had lost security, a best man at their weddings, a college graduate to look up to, to question. Perhaps those little black kids had even lost faith in the future, in education, or perhaps even part of themselves, their identity beyond being the brother of a brother who killed himself.

And Digger? In March, he lost everything but his mind, and even that hung in the balance above the abyss.

March had been one of Digger's favorite months, mainly because it housed Spring Break, a week off amidst the long spring semester, but partly too because the month winked warmth occasionally, flashes that revealed winter's demise. Although he loved snow in manageable amounts and in general preferred cold weather to warm, Digger enjoyed completions, time passages containing beginnings, middles, and endings that could be seen. The thought of a job that provided no finish was as abhorrent to the composition teacher as the Gomez' vehicle to the SS members. College semesters offered nice chunks of time, long enough in the middle months for the ends to feel like a well-earned reprieve. In terms of give and take, though, this March would be greedy.

He and Anna bickered. That was the right word for it, Digger admitted, and he thought of Thumb, the bitter brown liquid used to stop broken kids from being excited. Anna threw Thumb on his tongue, and he passed it back. Over nothing, they snapped at each other, over the amount of food in Shyla's bowl ("Cats like smaller meals," Digger knew.), the amount of salt Digger shook on his butter noodles ("It looks like snow," Anna complained.), over TV shows and noises made, over silence even. And Digger realized that not just Anna was to blame, for he could feel negativity rising—resentment, judgment, frustration, fear, and the worst of all: guilt—all the black emotions swirling deep within and wanting up and out, his dark river swelling to never-witnessed levels, over-flowing into consciousness even. Repeatedly, his mind returned to the grudge that Anna had not helped him cope with Danny, had not asked him the right questions (or almost any questions) to alleviate the demons that visited him nightly and told him how puny and weak and worthless he was, both he and Danny Jones, just fodder for the wind and the water, all that water. How could she not see how alone he was?

They hardly talked to each other, the cottage's silence no longer a harbor from a noisy world. Even the air itself tasted bitter, but maybe that was just the ocean's salt exhales. Maybe, *certainly*, everything was subjective, the mood a matter of vision, but Anna definitely went out more, asked him to join her less. Those were verifiable facts, not narrow-minded opinions. *A phase*, Digger told himself, the words becoming a mantra, one that smothered even the few syllables cast into the heavens by Danny Jones. Was Digger becoming the boy? Clearly reverting, Digger found some comfort in alcohol, and on weekend nights he would go through a six-pack of Bud, one after another, hiding the cans in the recycling bin so that Anna would not latch onto their number the second she came home—if she did.

On the Friday night before Spring Break, with nine days of irresponsibility (except for papers, always papers) within his vision, Digger watched the late news but couldn't have repeated any of the flashes of woe, sat and stared at David Letterman's monologue but heard no jokes, drank his fifth beer and began thinking of the sixth. At midnight, as in a fairy tale (one from Grimm), Anna returned. He had heard her tires crunching the driveway. Like a statue, he sat, faced the TV, waited.

Anna came through the back door, as they both usually did, and saw Digger on the couch. He had not turned to face her.

"What's on?" she said.

"Letterman."

"Who are the guests? she said, but Digger didn't know.

"You having some beers?"

"Bud kept me company." This answer displeased the woman, who made a noise and turned toward the bedroom. The ice in Digger's brain cracked a bit.

"Anna," said Digger, and he turned to see her backside (this time, she failed to face him). "We used to sing."

It was true. Throughout their five-year marriage and during their three-year "courtship," music had always flowed between them, connected them, lit up their union like a visible aura. Anna could remember all the lyrics to any song ever created, and Digger made up funny lyrics to ones that he could not remember. Sometimes, they would just make melodies out of la-la's. Digger had even known what their tombstone would tell the ages, planning to have a note chiseled into the stone's back "cover": "Listen, you can hear them sing." He had imagined cemetery visitors reading the two sentences (he didn't mind the comma splice!) and hearing the sunlight falling through the trees' golden branches, the orchestra of the birds, the turning earth. He clung to the certainty of this vision. During the long winter that had now flowed into March, Digger had pictured their tombstone often, a buoy in an ocean touched only by horizons.

They used to sing.

"I'm too tired, Matt," Anna had said, and to Digger it sounded sad, not defensive.

Digger was tired, too. He listened to Anna's using the bathroom and tried to watch Letterman. The late-night host and his sidekick, Paul Shaffer, seemed to be doing something funny, wearing sombreros and then riding donkeys, the long sweet ears of burrows, like furry corn husks. Digger swallowed the remaining beer—too warm!—and heard the finality of the bedroom's door clicking closed. The living room seemed huge and then tiny, expansive and then claustrophobic, as though the cottage were breathing. Digger thought about his gravestone—cold, gray, wordless on back.

Spring Break's conclusion actually lightened Digger's heart, for he found some solace by focusing on teaching (and even on his suspicions involving Mandy and her Nazi friend, Michael Kraft). Danny Jones still haunted the writing professor, too, even though the boy's face was dissolving into non-recognition. The topic of suicide still touched his assignments, even in his two 102 literature classes. For their third projects, Digger was having students analyze literary elements in a poem, "Richard Cory," by E. A. Robinson. In just four four-line stanzas, the poet poured metaphors, alliteration, symbols, irony, and imagery, giving students plenty of paragraphing choices. As an added bonus, students never seemed to had read the poem in high school, so Digger loved to present it aloud in class, to see their shock at the final stanza, the final line, when the rich Richard Cory, a man whom the poor speaker and his working-class peers idolized like royalty, like an angel, shot himself, the poet's using the phrase "put a bullet in his head" to show the character's strong intent, his suicidal will.

That Monday afternoon, in his second literature class, after Digger read the familiar lines and sixteen students (no absences, no family emergencies!) sat gaping, the composition instructor's mind transitioned from the sad hero, Richard Cory, to the fallen boy, Danny Jones. He had "put" himself on that high railing, "put" himself into the wind, into gravity. Or did "they" *put* him there? *The voices.* Were they his own? Where did schizophrenic voices originate? From the past, from the imagination, from Hell?

As he stood before the class amidst these misty thoughts, Anna appeared suddenly, too, strolling through the swirling vapor, and she looked like a ghost herself, unreachable. Digger focused himself back to the present, said to the class, "You didn't expect that, did you? Who knew that a poem could be so powerful!" Then he shifted the class toward their analytical essay: "Okay, let's generate some immediate feedback using ideas from our last project, language types. Descriptive, connotative, emotive. What types does Robinson use? Read over the poem again to see what you can see on first analysis."

As the sixteen students re-read "Richard Cory," Digger wrote "Robinson's language choices?" on the white board with a blue ink marker, and when everyone looked done with the poem, he explained the next exercise, free-writing.

"Let's do some free-writing, which you probably did in 101 or even in high school. Do you know how to free-write? Who can explain?"

As he asked, he had known that Mandy could explain since he had introduced the ideas-generating tactic in her 101 class and since she seemed pretty knowledgeable in general. Since identifying Michael Kraft as Mandy's friend (cohort?), Digger had replayed incidents from her class last semester, and he remembered one in particular, a subordination exercise in which Mandy had pointed him toward the Goths as Danny's antagonists. Had she been practicing misdirection? In that English 101 class, Digger remembered one student of color, a quiet girl named Leslie, and hadn't she and Mandy been paired together once? Had they worked well together? Digger's memory failed him there. As expected, she raised her hand partway and then started explaining: "Just write. On your paper or screen, just write. Don't think about grammar or spelling. Just let your thoughts out. Don't stop."

Could this student, who had learned so much, be one of the "they" who had pushed a fellow human being into nothingness? Could she have followed—or even led—a young white supremacist onto a teacher's property to deface it with Nazi symbols? Although Digger had trouble believing it, he had to find out.

"I couldn't describe it any better myself," said Digger, but then he did: "The 'don't stop' advice is especially important because free-writing can *free* you from the constraints of regular brainstorming or listing. Free-writing lets your mind flow into areas which regular conscious thoughts could miss. So if your mind draws a blank for a second or two, go back to this prompt [he gestured to the board], to 'Robinson's language choices,' to get you moving again. Some people call this tactic 'Hot Penning' because your pen should get hot with use. We're free-writing now just to do a quick reader response to see the first impressions that come out. Everybody ready? Got paper? If you'd rather, just type into your laptops. You might want to turn the screens off, too, so that you aren't tempted to stop and read what you wrote. Your goal is to keep the words, the ideas, flowing. Okay, ready? Free-write!"

As usual, Digger joined in, free-writing onto a piece of paper from his notebook, where he kept his classes' lesson plans so that he could glance at them and remember everything he wanted to do. Since he knew Robinson's poem so well, Digger's free-writing was rich with specific ideas, focusing on the juxtaposition of positive and negative words, on the flowing images of royalty in the first three stanzas and on the leaden weariness of the last four lines, on the savagery of the "put." To Digger, the words "put" and "pavement" (the latter used by the speaker to describe all the poor working slobs, himself included, who worshipped Richard Cory) offered the keys to unlocking the poem, and when he read it aloud, he emphasized the two "p" sounds to show the bitterness, the self-reflection of the characters, both the speaker and Richard Cory.

After half a page of scribbling quickly, Digger felt his wrist begin to protest, his forearm to freeze, his fingers to lock. Neither free-writing nor life itself were for the feint hearted. Reaching the bottom of the page at last, Digger stopped, flexed his right arm and hand, and watched most of his class still at it. A few students had stopped and were pretending that they had not. Mandy was frowning, then grinning, stabbing away at her notebook. Digger felt a little sorry for it, imagined the pages erupting into flames, maybe into swastikas and then fire. He would have to confront her, *maybe today*. Reluctance nagged, though. What would he say? How could he ask whether she was a Nazi wanabee? If he were not careful, Mandy could report him for harassment. She would, too; she was the outspoken type.

"Okay," he said. "That's probably enough. Free-writing's tough on your hand [students all around the room were flexing just as he had]. The next time we free-write, if we do, I'll probably have you read your writing in groups and present your analyses, maybe for our last paper, on your writing skills. For now, though, since I just wanted your first reactions to the poem, let's share your ideas as a class. First, read over your free-writing to yourself and circle what you might want to share."

Digger noticed that Mandy was smiling about something, thought it must be the word "share" (or perhaps the image of black crossed lines). In most classes, the same handful (or less) of students liked to share their opinions, the others not so much. Years ago, when Digger was a part-time teacher of 8 a.m. classes, he remembered Bill Jacobs' huffing into the Adjunct Faculty Office before class and announcing that he had no lesson plan ready, implying that he was not too worried about this lack of preparation. He had then followed this insanity with a statement that had stuck with Digger throughout all the days since: "I suppose I could just do a peer review or class discussion." Digger had laughed with Bill then, but ever since he had viewed both those exercises with suspicion, thinking of them as the "just" lesson plans and changing many of those exercises into more active, interesting ones. Waiting for his literature students to reply on a Monday late afternoon, Digger realized that he should probably have changed this little class discussion into some collaborative presentation, but then Mandy saved him.

"Richard Cory looked like a master but was really a slave," she said, surprising her teacher and no doubt most of her peers.

Nietzsche, thought Digger. *Masters and slaves.* Nazis!

"Nietzsche," he said. "Right? 'There are only masters and slaves.'"

Mandy declared that her philosophy teacher had taught them that last semester and that since then she had noticed the two poles everywhere.

"Why did you say 'looked like a master'?" asked Digger. "What words give the reader that impression?" he added to focus the whole class, hoping to snare another speaker.

Without pausing, though, Mandy listed some examples off without looking at the poem: "Glittered, fluttered, rich. His name is 'Richard,' you know, rich. That's symbolic."

"That seems likely and shows a nice quick analysis, descriptive words creating positive images, positive symbols, too. So why do you say that Richard Cory was actually a 'slave'? What words suggest that?" He had looked from Mandy to the whole class, sweeping across all the faces, suggesting that the class discussion branch out. No branches sprouted any leaves, though, any blossoms. *All dead wood.* Digger thought again of his mistake in lesson plans, of the need for collaborative, active exercises.

Time passed because this time Mandy had had to look at the poem and use her teacher's question to dig away for an answer. Everybody searched the poem, but Mandy uncovered an opinion and held it up first: "The last stanza," she declared.

"What words?" Digger wanted to show students the power of specifics—both points and proof.

Although he had directed the question to the whole class again, hoping somewhat hopelessly to snare another volunteer, Mandy said without looking up, "Worked, waited, went without. A lot of 'w' words."

"Too many for coincidence, right, Mandy?" said Digger, turning back to the student leader. "So Robinson meant to use those 'w' words, and that's called alliteration, by the way, the same sound beginnings. Why did the poet want that sound?"

At last, the conversation caught on, another student, another girl, adding, "'Went home' ... and 'one calm summer night.' Oh, wait, that's an 'o' word."

"But it sounds like a 'w' one, Jess, so that's more proof that Robinson was up to something, maybe something to do with Mandy's 'slave' point. Why do you think Robinson repeated that letter so much in the last stanza?"

Nobody knew, not even Jess or Mandy, whose lips were twisted and head cocked as she tried to wrestle the answer from the computer screen (Digger had posted the poem on the course site). Then Digger read the four lines again, stressing the w's, drawing them out.

"I know!" cried Mandy. "That's why Richard Cory's a slave. All the w's sound tired, like he's weary. He's weak like a slave, wasted. The 'w' words show that Richard Cory's not a master."

Getting so specific so soon like this was a great start, yet Digger worried that Mandy's peers would just use her analysis in their papers, not really understanding it or taking the time to find their own reasoning. Of course, that theft could occur after group work, too, but at least then more students would have volunteered their thoughts, creating more of a group effort rather than this almost individual one. So Digger decided to transition a bit, to give students ideas for their essays' beginning and endings, which didn't have to focus on Robinson's language but could instead lead readers to ponder life, death, the mysteries.

"Can Cory really be classified as a master or a slave? Can you define anyone as either extreme?" He hoped that Mandy would not respond too soon, that his questions would have time to sink and ferment a bit, especially the second one.

Neither did. "I can," spoke Mandy, and for once Digger was a little bothered by the leader who had followed him from one class to the next and who had been a great help with his collaborative lessons—and who had painted six swastikas on the side of his house?

He held up a finger to ask that she wait, but he saw in all the other faces that his definition questions had burst already, that they had floated away in fragments. Everyone just wanted to know what Mandy would say. *At least*, the teacher thought, *they're not looking into their laps*, the telltale sign of cell phone abuse.

"Okay," he said to Mandy, smiling (for he did appreciate her enthusiasm). "Who's a master, to start?"

Her answer surprised him and made everybody else laugh (and caused him not to ask a follow-up about slaves).

Perfectly at ease, chin up, bronze Mandy said, "I am."

At home, alone as usual, Digger listened to the wind, looked for his lost cat (searched less and less, though), and thought about Mandy's self-declared "mastery." He had not asked her why, instead treating her arrogance as though it were humorous and transitioning the class back to the poem, regretting his tangent. Mandy had represented success for Digger, a student who retained what he taught and passed it on to peers, but was she something else? Bronzed like a Roman statue, yet the Goths had toppled those, right? Digger had hardly thought of those black crows this semester, had never even spotted one of those black-clad boys or girls with a vampire's make-up. Goth students had obviously not driven Danny to suicide; they just looked wrong, out of place. But what if another group looked right but did wrong? His mind went back to a focusing exercise from weeks past: the SS. *Nazis at OVC*! Gwena would hate that, worrying that she might be taken for their faculty advisor. Nobody would do that, all because of a nickname. *Mandy ... Amanda.* Wasn't that a Jewish name? Digger didn't know.

He couldn't sleep at night, too many images and words churning in his mind. Outside the cottage, the bay breezes swirled and swept the beaches clear of snow, and inside, Digger tossed and turned and began leaving Anna's side at midnight so that he didn't keep her up or wake her. Out on the couch, he would toss and turn and listen to the winds, external and internal.

He felt like Dorothy in the tornado, his mind's eye the window where everything and everyone sailed past, Anna on a bike and waving (good-bye?), Skittles as Toto, shadows that took shape (almost), Danny's falling, his eyes.

One Sunday morning in late March, Digger stumbled from the couch to find Anna seated in the kitchen. Beside her, like a fat seeing-eye dog, squatted her big blue suitcase.

"Going somewhere?" said Digger.

He could tell that Anna was serious, that what she had to say and do had been thought out, planned, because she looked directly into his eyes and delivered words with no gaps between them, no hesitations. And she used his name repeatedly, nailing the statements into reality.

"Matt," she began, "I need some time by myself, so I'm going away for now. I need to think about my life, about what I want and need."

"I know what I need," said Digger.

"You think you do," answered his wife. "But you have your work. That's what you need. And coffee," she added before he could speak. He did need coffee.

As she poured him a cup from their little four-cup machine, Digger asked her about Shyla, as though she had not just informed him that she was leaving, going away. *A phase, a phase.* Yet after she placed the cup before him, she continued in that vein: "Matt, you have your job right now. You are your job. You might not see it, but since becoming full-time, you've been pretty obsessed. You work all the time, seven days a week. You even come home during the week and work sometimes, revising lesson plans and reading scholarly articles, writing reviews, researching, checking OVC for pre-requisites, career paths."

Digger felt defensive and started to repeat those excuses, all the planning and committee work, the advisees, who weren't even his actual students, but Anna cut him off, having heard all the burdens before.

"We've actually been separated for over two years now."

Separated?

"I don't want to be separated," said Digger softly, staring into the rising and disappearing steam from his coffee. *Everything disappears.*

"Right now," said Anna, softly, too, "I need to be by myself, Matt. As you can see, I packed what I need, and I'm going to stay with Carrie for a while. You have work. Today, you'll be doing online papers, and tomorrow, you'll have more."

Carrie's fault, thought Digger, and then, "Papers!"

"Are the Celtics on tonight or tomorrow?" she asked, but he didn't answer. He didn't know.

"I'll keep in touch and let you know what's going on. You don't need to worry about me, Matt."

What about me?

"I fed Shyla while you were sleeping. She almost let me pet her. You'll be able to pet her soon, and maybe Skittles will come back. Tell the cats that I'll miss them."

What about me?

"I'll miss you, too, Matt, but this is something that I need to do. You wouldn't want me to stay and feel resentful. I just feel a little trapped, Matt, and I need to figure things out. I've been thinking of my father a lot, of his motivation. I've seen his life only from my mother's point of view, and that was biased." She paused then and started again: "If we're meant to continue, Matt, we will. I used to feel free, not free from you. I used to feel free with you, but I don't right now, for whatever reason. My work, my past. I want to feel free again."

Digger mainly heard two words, "trapped" and "free." They stoked a pilot light of righteousness, a mix of defensiveness and anger. In his mind, he put out the little flame before it could really ignite. He watched the steam climb up the inner side of his coffee cup and then reach into the air for a few inches before vanishing. The sinuous probing conjured the image of pathetic earthworms twisting away from OVC's concrete walkways, and then Digger thought of Richard Cory, of the two hard "p" words, "pavement" and "put." He had no energy to argue, especially when this kitchen scene could not be real, had to be a phase.

"I'm going now," Anna said, and she pushed her chair back, its quick scream awakening Digger immediately. Anna was standing; she was leaving.

"Anna," he said, looking up at her. He had not even sipped his coffee. "Please don't go" and then, "Please come back."

"For now, I need to go." Her eyes swam (a light green in the shadowed kitchen), her light hair fluttered, as though nature itself were giving the scene a theatrical flair. She had reached the back door, and her suitcase must have been heavy because it caused her to tilt a bit and to grasp it with both hands. She looked out the door into the future, a Matt-less path.

"Shyla's here," she said, the words wobbling in a mix of emotions impossible to decipher and control. "Bye, Matt."

She used the door, cooed at the cat with non-words, and then he heard the Honda awaken, the tires grinding away, away. Digger sat and stared at his coffee, heard his black river gurgle and flow, sensed a flashflood, drowning. Then he steadied his mind. Maybe Anna was right, for suddenly he felt almost glad to be by himself.

Shyla was here. In a minute, he would get up, go out, and pet the wild cat. He raised the coffee cup to his lips and found that its contents were cold.

Chapter Fourteen: Description

For most college essays, description is superfluous, beyond the paper's purpose, except for Art students, of course, who often have to describe a work in meticulous detail to get at the artistic principles communicated, such as balance and harmony, perhaps discord. Basically, their paragraphs structured around Description act like a mix between Classification (some division of a visual element, such as color) and Illustration (the specific details). Education majors might also have to describe a classroom when doing a real-world observation, and engineers and architects might be required to describe machinery and entire buildings, but in general this structural plan in academia is somewhat rare.

Digger slept on the couch now, every night. The bedroom was too small, dark, and empty, and it was Anna's room, would be kept *as is* until her return. In the living room, Digger felt more positioned in the center of things, had more space around him, could hear the ocean, the winds tapping at the widows, could see little lights on distant shores, not just his nearby neighbors beyond the fences. On the couch, he could actually sleep a bit, the turbulence inside ironically lessened now that what he had most feared had actually happened. *A phase, though*, and he pounded away at that word, dulled it. *This was Anna's home, too.* Hers, his, and Shyla's (*what about Skittles?*).

As April trod on, one Anna-less day after another (she had not kept in touch, but she had returned for more of her stuff one day when he was at OVC. She had left him a note telling him what she took and added that she was doing "good thinking"), Digger began to sit out on the little porch as Shyla ate, talking to her and reaching out a hand. Even on cold days, he sat wrapped and told Shyla how pretty she was and how Skittles would soon return. At first, the cat would glance suspiciously up at Digger after each bite—ready for flight—but within a couple of weeks after Anna's departure, he had been able to touch the little black back without Shyla's springing away. Digger felt her backbone and the way Shyla pushed up at his touch, warmth communicated on both sides. With that physical connection, the two creatures turned a corner, for by mid-April, Digger was actually petting the little cat's glossy black fur, the short hair feeling like velvet over the ridges of her spine. And on sunny days (not too many of those in April, another of New England's more bipolar months in terms of temperature), Digger noticed a brush of brown in Shyla's black coat, almost crimson, a heat that rose too through her golden eyes, which would focus on Digger to find his essence, discover it suddenly (a small, safe pulsing, not so dissimilar from her own), and blink slowly, giving him an "Anna kiss," as he labeled it, winking slowly back at the little animal, thinking of what he had gained and what he had lost. Soon, anyway, he would be able to pick Shyla up, cradle her against his chest. *Small things!*

His sub-conscious thoughts were less positive, for throughout the night, the dreams came. Perhaps because he found sleep sooner now, Digger was able to sink more quickly into the fictional realm and reach that level where the dark tales could slither, grow, and rise. In these nightmares, Anna played a prominent role, of course, as did the looming Bay Bridge, the winds, the darkness, the little pricks of stars, crying in their retreat. Sometimes Anna would be up on the rail, serene, though, and unreachable, but usually it was Danny, who looked like the stereotypical silent-movie "negro" with wide white eyes and dark, dark skin, a "yes'ser mastuh" oval-mouthed expression. As the reel of this dream played out again and again, the same emotions tripped over themselves—fear, impotence, frustration, anger, fear. The boy shone with terror, and Digger, clutched by a nightmare that he had actually lived, had become just another extension of that great fear. The wind ripped and tore at them! Danny would be staring down at him, beseeching him somehow, and then— woooop!—he would fly and hover, like the coyote who had just walked off the cliff with an Acme anvil in his arms, hover and drop in a flash. *Gone.* Darkness and silence and no air, all wind but no air, a tornado of sound amidst absolute stillness, and in the dream Digger would think of a hurricane's eye, and rising from the unconscious slumber, he would realize that the sound came not from his brain but from his blood, pulsing and hammering through his own body.

He would awaken on his couch in his living room, in the darkness, the silence, alone.

In these nightmares, only Danny jumped. Anna would just perch atop the rail, her light hair flowing through the night, her eyes glowing green in the darkness, the stars just extensions of her inner beauty. Every so often, Digger would dream himself atop the rail—no Anna, no Danny—with stars flecked far above, dark waters glistening far below, and when he would awaken from this dream, the composition instructor would feel at peace.

No Goths ever materialized in Digger's dreams, and thankfully no Nazis, either.

Once, Shyla appeared in his dream bridge world, the two of them below the railing and just looking down as time passed, two who were alike now, two left-behind creatures. Both alone yet together on a stony narrow path, the heavens yawning above, the abyss whispering below.

April brought not only dreams and spring showers but two uncomfortable conversations (confrontations?). With the semester grinding toward its conclusion, Digger knew that he had to find out about Mandy, not only for Danny Jones, but for himself. He had to discover if this somewhat rare student leader had a dark side, a particularly shadowed one. And with Anna gone, he had to accomplish something, had to care about someone else, had to escape himself and the deep hole that had engulfed him.

One Friday after the day's last class drew to a close, Digger asked Mandy (as she stowed her laptop into a backpack) for "a word," saying that he "needed her help with a problem." After the other students left and Mandy was standing before his desk, looking open and unconcerned, waiting with a small smile for this "problem," Digger hesitated because he wasn't quite sure what to say. As his suspicions and the past weeks had played out, he had decided not to confront her directly. *But how to begin?*

"Your friend Michael," he started, noticing that his star student's smile suddenly flattened, that her eyes narrowed. She looked anything but open and unconcerned now.

"Michael?" she said, as though to finish Digger's beginning. "He's no friend of mine."

"Your old friend, then," continued Digger. "I was hoping that you could help me with something I heard. I heard that this Michael, Michael Kraft, has an affinity for German history, for Nazis, in fact, and as you might know, my house had swastikas painted onto it."

"I had nothing to do with that," the girl said quickly. "I didn't even know about it," she added. Mandy was no longer looking at him, Digger noticed. The door seemed to fascinate his student, along with the floor, the walls. She looked pale, too, and Digger thought ironically of the Goths, whom Mandy had tried to implicate last fall. Digger thought "misdirection" and kept himself on the lookout for tangents.

"Other swastikas have appeared on campus," Digger said, and Mandy stared at the ceiling (looking for answers from above?). "So anyone who seems attracted to Nazis would be a likely suspect, right?"

Mandy nodded a few times, glancing at Digger, at the floor, at the walls. Digger wondered if the walls seemed to be closing in, yet he wasn't sure if Mandy had played a part in the vandalism, let alone Danny's suicide. Those two subjects still seemed likely to be unrelated. Michael, though—this girl knew that he was guilty and by extension, she herself.

"Mandy, I don't suspect you. You're a great student, and I've been privileged to have you in both required writing classes. However, I have to ask, I need to know, were you involved in any of these vandalism incidents with Michael Kraft?"

The troubled girl said, "No" so quickly that Digger actually heard, "Yes," but how could he prove it?

"I can't speak for Michael," she continued, "because we haven't been friends for months now, since last semester. Michael's a little crazy, a little right wing. Listen, he's no Nazi, I don't know who's been saying what, but he is a little crazy. He ..." But Mandy didn't finish that thought.

Digger said, "You should talk to your old friend, Mandy, and help him if he needs help. The vandals, whoever they are, will get caught. They'll get prosecuted, at least kicked out of school. Swastika graffiti is no doubt a hate crime."

"I don't hate anybody," said Mandy quickly, and she glanced again at Digger, met his eyes for a moment before severing the connection. "I just want to do well," she continued. "Haven't I done well in your class?"

Ah, misdirection again. "As I said, you have been and are a great student."

"And you still think that I vandalized your house?" she accused.

"No," said Digger, but what he thought was, *Yes, you did it. You and rich Michael Kraft and probably that big-headed guy and maybe others, other little fascists*. After all, six swastikas had been stuck on his house—six vandals? Or maybe three, each responsible for two of the Nazi symbols.

"Funny thing was," he said, thinking of those six black swastikas, "one of the swastikas was painted backwards," and for an instant Digger saw arrogance and anger gleam from his student's eyes, which had rolled up almost imperceptibly. He imagined that both his mind and Mandy's were focused on the same person: Big Head.

Color had resurfaced into Amanda Jenkins' face. She looked directly at Digger and said, "You know me, Professor Diggerson. I wouldn't make a stupid mistake like that."

Digger shook his head up and down a few times, a little bobble, for *yes*, he knew her, at least now he did.

The second unappetizing conversation grew from the first, which bothered Digger almost as much as Anna's disconnection from him (or maybe the Mandy talk was just a distraction, his own misdirection). For a week, Digger debated disclosing his recent student information with someone, any school authority. One side of his mind said that he had no proof, only a pair of names and suspicions, nothing that could be added to a record, nothing that could be recorded at all. But knowledge made Digger feel culpable. Another voice unearthed a series of disquieting questions: What if something else happened? What if Mandy and Michael and Big Head were to blame for the rash of Nazi propaganda? Even worse, for he had not forgotten Danny Jones, what if they—the SS—had been the "they" who had bullied the boy into jumping from the Bay Bridge? The bridge was still there, waiting. What if other students were in danger?

Realizing that he did in fact have to talk to someone at OVC, at least to cover his own "ass," Digger first thought of Gwena. She was, after all, his department's leader, but this issue was not an academic one. He would just be passing his responsibility to her, and that transfer would not be fair. Yet thinking of Gwena led him to another face, a round one, the "host" of Danny's memorial, Omar Johns. Therefore, after classes and his office hour, late in April, Digger walked up the long sidewalk to the Administration Building, where once he had passed a solitary Danny Jones and a group of possible Nazis, searched down a quiet, wood-paneled, first-floor hallway, found the name *Omar Johns* on a bronze plaque beside a mahogany door, and knocked twice. Silence. Then Digger heard a chair bark and two muffled words: "Come in."

Digger did as told. He had never officially met Omar Johns, never even talked to him, so he was surprised that the man was short (he must have been standing on something at Danny's memorial) and that he was smiling as though greeting an old friend. *Salesman,* Digger thought, but he said instead, "Mr. Johns?"

"Doctor Johns," corrected the man, his smile unwavering, and then he added, his finger pointing and shaking at Digger a bit, as though to place him correctly, "and you are Professor ... Diggerson. Humanities. Composition." At Digger's raised eyebrows, the administrator laughed and then continued, "No, we have never met, but I make it a point to know all of my faculty members, and you, Professor Diggerson, are quite famous all by yourself, are you not? A good reputation and of course all that bad press involving the unfortunate suicide and vandalism. Why even your own house was vandalized."

Digger had found this summary to be a bit unnerving, reminding him of Big Brother, so he took advantage of the administrator's last reference and pause to get right to the point: "That's why I'm here, Doctor Johns. I might have some information, at least about the vandalism." At this, Johns nodded sagely and lowered himself back into his green-leather chair.

"Please continue."

"From a pair of my own students, I have learned about a student group of Nazis, Nazi wanabees anyway, and that seems too coincidental with all the swastikas that have arisen lately." Johns nodded—*please continue.*

"Well," said Digger, "as I said, I might know who the vandals are, but I have no proof, just a pair of names and my own investigations, my own suspicions."

Omar Johns said nothing, but reached into his desk's top side drawer and extracted a small notebook. Then he reached toward Digger but instead plucked an expensive-looking pen from its silver holder, the mouth of a horse's severed head. Digger watched these acts and waited, suspecting that he was supposed to wait. Then the man with the incredibly round head spoke again: "We need to back up, Professor Diggerson. You lost me with all these mentions of students. Let us go from point A to point B, or to whatever point we have arrived at right now."

Digger had known professors—knew them—who acted calm and controlled like this. He distrusted them. "I have no proof," the teacher repeated, "but I feel that I must go on record with my suspicions in case something else happens."

"Let us begin with these names."

Digger was reminded of a doctor waiting for a list of symptoms. When Omar Johns looked up at him, no doubt to urge these names into being, Digger thought that Anna would call the administrator's round head "cute," or in the past she would have. The man's features were spread out in a balanced way.

"Two possible student vandals," Digger finally said. "One is a student of mine—a really good student, by the way, all A's, a hard grade to get from an English teacher—and the other is a supposed friend of hers. I've heard from another of my students that the latter is part of a group called the SS, a reference to Nazi Germany, of course, and this student—the Nazi, not the one who told me about him—his name is Michael Kraft. I saw this Michael with one of my own students last semester, an Amanda Jenkins, the 'A' writer."

After all these words, Digger realized that the administrator had written down just four: "Michael Kraft" and "Amanda Jenkins." So Digger started talking again, going back to last October, mentioning Danny Jones but staying focused mainly on the vandalism, filling in Johns on the chronology of his suspicions. Concluding, Digger said again, "I obviously have no proof beyond my one student and my own observations. But I think that these two students are our vandals—and maybe worse."

Johns ignored the "worse" implication, responding, "The vandalism was a black eye for OVC [Digger thought, *What about Danny's suicide?*], but you do realize that I cannot take any action on your information, for as you say, you have no proof. Accusations require evidence, or they could lead to lawsuits. Presumed innocent, Professor Diggerson, correct?"

"Yes," said Digger, but he did think that the administrator could at least check Michael's and Mandy's student records, perhaps talk to their Resident Advisors or academic ones, maybe a professor or two. Digger kept these suggestions to himself.

"Is there anything else, Professor Diggerson?"

He was getting the bum's rush, the salesman's dismissal (upon realizing that the customer would be no buyer). "No," he said reluctantly, rising from the visitor's chair (also green leather—*soft, nice*). Johns rose, too, and thanked Digger and shook his hand. It was a nice shake, not too soft, not too long. Probably Johns had learned how to shake hands in some administrators' class.

"I expect that these vandalism incidents are at an end," said Omar Johns, and when Digger exited the Admin Building and felt the refreshing spring promise of a late-April late afternoon, he thought so, too.

They had found the administrator's name online, on the Ocean View College website, a whole line of grinning old white men, one with a particularly big, stupid round head.

"Look at that," Mandy had said, laughing at the screen, which showed head shots of a dozen smiling

OVC administrators. "Omar Johns! His head touches both sides of the picture, it's so round!"

"A Jew name and a Jew head," said the SS leader, Michael Kraft.

"Why do we hate Jews, Mike?" asked Shrek. His own head looked pretty large, so that "No-Neck" would have been another appropriate nickname, one that he would have liked even less than Shrek. He had gotten used to Shrek, grown into it.

The only members of the eight in this gathering were Shrek, Mandy, and Michael, the others all declining the opportunity to put a slash through the circled "Round headed Jew Administrator" from the List (now identified as Doctor Omar Johns). None of the other five had liked the leader's plan, and most had been tiring of the game anyway, especially with final exams coming in a few weeks. Shrek had decided to go only to show an absence of fear, which he felt keenly but tried to hide behind questions. He had forgotten why the administrator's name was even listed, other than his being a Jew, of course.

And of course Mandy had told Michael about her professor's suspicions, about his knowing Michael's name (she had not mentioned her disowning of her friend, though), but the SS leader had laughed off the threat. "What does Diggerson know?" he had boasted, adding "Stupid Jew!"

"He's mostly Scottish," Mandy had corrected him, whereupon Michael Kraft had announced, "A Scottish Jew then. They're all over the place, like a plague."

Mandy had recognized the logic in his point. Of course, Jews had spread all over the place. That was the problem. She had added, "They probably spread the plague with their own dirty feet," and Michael had enjoyed that idea.

"Jews think they're the chosen ones," said Michael, but Shrek didn't know what this meant.

"They think they're masters," said Mandy, not helping the big-headed follower either.

"And they killed Jesus," added Michael, a point that connected with the other male, who thought, *They did?*

"They're just slaves," said Mandy.

The leader liked that. "Just slaves!" he repeated.

Slaves? "Like blacks?" said Shrek.

Michael laughed at that (he was always laughing). "White blacks!" he declared.

Shrek decided not to pursue this line of conversation. "The Jews killed Jesus," he told himself on his path through the night. The three were taking a long-cut through one of OVC's back parking lots, a smaller one since it allowed only faculty and staff, no students. At this late hour, faculty and staff were all gone, and it was almost pleasant walking with his friends, thought Shrek. *Just a little scary.* They were headed for the rear of the Administration Building because, as Michael had said, that's where the Jew Johns had an office. Okay, that was understandable enough. The three had left all truncheons in Michael and Shrek's dorm room (they were roomies), and only Mandy held anything, a dark backpack, which she had looped around one shoulder since only nerds strapped both to their backs.

Since the Administration Building's back door was illuminated, the three shadows stopped and stood just outside the bowl of light cast from the alcove above the entrance. The three waited for Michael.

"We need to take care of that light," said Michael, so Mandy un-slung the backpack, zipped it open, and handed out three of the spray paint cans that had been used at Digger's. Shrek yanked at his but couldn't get the top off.

"Squeeze the sides," said Mandy impatiently.

"And shake the bastards," added Michael. The darkness click-clacked, click-clacked, click-clacked with the unmistakable sound of spray paint being revved up.

"Get the light first," said Michael, and they advanced together into the cone of illumination, looked up, didn't notice the surveillance camera because of the light's glare, and blasted away, eclipsing the sun.

"That'll teach it," said Shrek because he wanted to say something, but neither Michael nor Mandy responded. Shrek was used to that.

"Okay," came Michael's voice from the sudden darkness (Shrek blinked his eyes for better viewing). "You two do the swastikas, and for God's sake, Shrek, you dyslexic bastard, make the points go clock-wise this time."

"I know," said Shrek, and then he said it again. But still he focused on the imagistic word, "clock-wise," as he sprayed the crossed Nazi lines. He had found out about Nazis, sort of, from the others and from the Web. The swastikas had appealed to him, but he had to admit that he had trouble remembering which way they rolled. *Clock-wise!*

Mandy finished first, then Shrek, and they both watched Michael's painting words, big ones. Acclimated to the dark now, Shrek and Mandy read, "Jew Jons Go Home."

"You forgot the 'h,'" said Mandy, giggling. She had felt nerves rippling and was trying to keep them hidden beneath sound.

Michael had trouble reading what he had written because of the darkness and his proximity to the door, so he stepped back, screwed up his eyes a bit, and could see one "H." "What 'h'?" he said, feeling a little foolish and not liking that brush of heat. "There's an 'h,'" he added defensively.

"The 'h,'" said Shrek, and he laughed, too, mainly because Mandy was still giggling and because the sound broke the fear.

"You don't know what 'h,' moron!" said Michael, a little louder than he meant to be. He tended to lash out when needing to gain equilibrium.

"The 'h,'" said Shrek defensively.

"Johns," said Mandy clearly because she had achieved emotional control and stopped laughing. "The 'h' between 'o' and 'n'."

Shit!" Michael said, as though blaming the administrator's name, and he bent forward and added a squat "h" as best he could. It floated above its neighboring letters.

"Looks like an 'n,' not an 'h,'" said Shrek.

"Shut up!" said Michael.

Mandy said nothing. She thought it was funny when Michael yelled at Shrek, who was definitely a dumb ass and deserved it. She never knew how he had even gotten accepted into this private college, which was too good for him. Ignoring the two squabbling males, Mandy bent forward, too, and added two curving letters beneath Michael's declaration as a signature: SS.

Michael seemed pleased since he laughed shortly and then said, "Let's go!" Adrenaline pumped through the leader's system, dispelling the recent defensiveness and drowning all fear.

Their dorm waited down by the top of the campus, past the last academic building, the one for faculty offices, and they moved through the night toward it. Nobody said anything until Shrek, who was uncomfortable during stretches of silence, asked, "What's 'SS' again?"

Mandy scoffed silently and let Michael answer since she could never remember how to pronounce, let alone spell, the German word, all those syllables slurring about.

"Schwaden Schwarden," said Michael, accenting the "Schward."

"Schwaden Schwarden?" repeated Shrek, stressing the "den."

"Oh, God!" said Mandy. "You're both not pronouncing it right."

"Isn't that the beginning of that old rock song," Shrek laughed. "You know, the one about 'burning out' and 'fading away.' Schweeden Schwarden Schwooden."

"What the hell are you talking about, Shrek?" said Michael.

"That old song," said Shrek defensively.

"The SS," Mandy told him, "were the elite Nazi soldiers from World War Two. Just like we're the elite from this school and will be elite business leaders after it."

Both males approved of this little speech, nodding in the dark, and Mandy continued: "Our SS also means Suicide Squad because we want everyone on our list to jump off that bridge, just like Danny Jones."

Shrek walked in the shadows and looked up at the Bay Bridge, shining through the sky over this end of campus. Up close, it looked like a medieval castle.

"Who's Danny Jones?" he said.

May arrived with reddish buds on the maple trees, a hint of yellow brushing the forsythia bushes, yet winter stayed in Digger's heart. He didn't mind that, liked it actually, enjoyed cool air and the untouched innocence of snowfall, the curling wind-driven snow devils moving across the beach, the gulls like buoys scattered throughout the cold sand. And, of course, Anna lived in the winter cottage, an image that Digger nourished, sometimes with the help of Budweiser.

In the kitchen's miscellaneous drawer, he had found an old note (must have fallen in) from Anna this past winter. "Gone to do errands," it read. No names. No "love." But it was Anna's swirling script, so Digger kept that one in the drawer and sometimes put it on the table, propped up by the salt shaker so that he could read it at a glance. Focusing on it while drinking coffee, he would imagine that she had just written it that morning, that the "errands" were her "phase" and that she would come through the back door later that day, bearing a smile and perhaps a Mario's pizza. Digger had not enjoyed one of those in months because he never drove over the bridge now, the memory too raw still. Why remind him of something that he couldn't forget anyway?

Did he even want to forget this past painful half year or more? Not when he had recently had a full life, not when memories could keep that life inflated, breathing.

One May weekend morning, Digger looked out the back window (over the sink) and saw that spring had definitely sprung. The sands showed no white patches, not even up into the sea grass, which glowed a bit now, too, more golden than the slumbering brown stalks of April. Digger even saw some green patches in his sandy back yard, and the old rhododendron bushes' sparse leafing seemed infused with a green sheen by nature's promise of warmth. But where was Shyla? *Where was Shyla?* That thought struck Digger like the iron tolling of a church bell, for every morning he would find her on or around the back steps, waiting for breakfast, looking up at the door. Today, the steps led down to nothing but those green smudges. *She must be in the crate*, Digger thought, and he immediately pushed open the door to call her name, to see the black and white flash run to him, to blink slowly into her golden eyes.

"Tsk, tsk, Shyla," he called, over and over, at least a dozen times, and while the sun caressed the bay and softened its winds, Shyla did not appear. She was gone, too.

Chapter Fifteen: Conclusions

An essay's final paragraph, usually the shortest one, still requires planning. If you want readers to keep your paper in mind, to ponder it, you can't bore them with your last handful of sentences, so remember the acronym BEST: Bookend by going back to the idea that started the paper, Extend by reaching beyond the thesis, and/or Summarize Thoughts by repeating the composition's thesis and topic sentences ideas, the main focuses. While a conclusion does not need all three tactics, often the ST content can begin the final paragraph, thus creating a transition from the last body paragraph, and then you can shift into the B information by referencing your hook/tease idea from the essay's first sentences, perhaps a startling statistic, thought-provoking quotation, or interesting analogy. From there, you could flow into E content by dealing with the paper's topic's larger issue, maybe by asking a probing question or two. Consequently, with the rearranged BEST, you will have led the audience out of your essay, but not out of their thoughts.

Despite the young year's losses, the tragedies without end, mid-May brought two satisfying conclusions: one to the long spring semester's classes, the other to the academic year's mystery of sporadic vandalism, at least the episodes involving spray paint.

The three students caught on the Administration Building's surveillance camera were finally identified by an R.A., the Resident Advisor from the three's dormitory. Ignorant of the part he had played, Digger knew nothing of Omar Johns' order for his secretary to locate the Resident Advisors for sophomore Michael Kraft and freshman Amanda Jenkins, who turned out to reside in the same dorm. The day before final exams, called Study Day, the three vandals were ordered to their R.A.'s suite on the dorm's first floor, and unsuspecting, confident, bordering on cocky, Michael, Mandy, and Shrek (the latter being mainly confused) walked into a room full of old men with stern faces, none of whom were recognizable. One was an administrator (not the targeted Johns), another the head of Campus Security (a retired OVPD cop who rarely left the guard house at the mouth of the campus' main entrance), and a third turned out to be a student advocate from Student Affairs, present for the three students' benefit but appearing more like a foe than a friend (due to age and attitude—i.e., gray hair and compressed lips). The administrator did most of the interrogating.

"You three have been called to this meeting about the recent vandalism at the Administration Building." The old man looked at each student for a full two seconds, moving his head as he focused in on each young face. He looked like an old clock, ticking. In Michael, the gray-haired gentleman saw arrogance; in Mandy, confidence; in Shrek, not much.

"Why call us?" said Michael.

The grandfatherly man sighed. "The back of Administration has a hidden surveillance camera. You three were identified by your Resident Advisor as you painted over the outdoor light. After that, the camera still picked up what you did, the resulting spray-painted vandalism, even though it was very dark." As he spoke, the old man had motioned toward the R.A., a senior, who was not part of the interrogation team and who was pretending to do work at his desk against the far wall. Michael, Mandy, and Shrek all followed the old man's gesture and stared at the R.A., their expressions unchanging.

"It wasn't us," said Mandy.

"We have the tape," said the administrator, sounding sad, disappointed. "I'm afraid there is no doubt."

Michael shifted tactics: "It was no big deal. It was a prank. My father will pay for any damage."

"Oh, I am sure of that," said the gray-haired fellow, suddenly much less sorrowful. "But as you know, this was not the first episode of vandalism on campus— even off it—so this goes beyond simple repayment. Vandalism of this nature damages our Ocean View community. It cannot, and will not, be tolerated."

Mandy, ever quick, saw the direction of things, and said, "We will apologize."

The administrator swiveled his head to face her, Mandy thinking that he looked a lot like a turtle, and said to the girl, "Again, this goes beyond an apology. This sort of hate speech is ..." The old man could not seem to find a word.

"It wasn't hate speech," said Michael and Mandy quickly, the mixture of voices sounding almost melodious.

The man from Student Affairs stepped forward, half a step, saying "You will, of course, get due process. A week from today, after final exams, we will meet at a tribunal to discuss the matter further and to determine consequences. Whatever those may be, you will have the opportunity to finish this spring semester."

In response to this lawyerly declaration, the three students had no words.

"What we still need to discover here," said the administrator, "is who else will stand before the Disciplinary Committee. So, who wants to tell me? Who else was part of your little spray-painting club?"

"Uh," said Shrek.

"Nobody else," said Michael.

"It was a one-time … thing," said Mandy.

"A dare," said Michael.

"We dared each other, us three," said Mandy.

"Uh," said Shrek.

The administrator aimed his turtle head at Shrek and wondered how this foolish boy had ever gotten admitted to their fine institution. He hoped to rectify that mistake in a week.

The week of finals—anxiety, fear, relief, and then a dull worry over grades, all four phases repeated for each exam—became history, and the three students were duly expelled by the Disciplinary Committee. Loyal to the end, though, Michael and Mandy named no names, and Shrek stayed mute, too, blinking and mumbling. When asked by the head of the tribunal (no less than Omar Johns himself) why they had painted swastikas, Michael had said that they were copycatting the earlier vandalism (Mandy's idea), which they had learned about not from other students, but from the administration's emails (Michael's idea). When questioned about the off-campus swastikas (at Digger's), all three students shook their heads, feigning ignorance (quite easy for Shrek, whose actual name was Joe), and when Omar Johns mentioned the tag "SS" at the Admin Building, Michael said nothing, Mandy offered, "It went with the swastikas," and Shrek volunteered, "They killed Jesus." It was his only statement during the entire proceeding, which never once included the name Danny Jones. These foolish young adults had had nothing to do with the lonely boy.

While no-news-is-bad-news might fit most money-making businesses, OVC's administrators disagreed with that philosophy, so they kept the disciplinary meeting and its decisions in-house. In another mass email to the OVC community, they provided sparse details (certainly no names) but heavy warnings by stressing the expulsion of the three vandals.

So, thought Digger as he read the interesting email, the SS did not drive Danny up the bridge, nor did a flock of non-conformist gothic pretenders push him off. Who did? *Who knows?* Real-life stories do not offer neat conclusions, tales to be tied prettily in ribbons and bows. No doctor could sum up the boy's reasoning, not even from an MRI, which might show lighted brain sections, dark ones, but no certainty beyond "This shows pleasure" and "This shows pain." Not even Doctor Joan Powers had the answers in her rigid little body. The only certainty was that Danny's mother, who looked like his older sister, now prayed above empty soil, but how was that any different for all the other mourners, the wives, fathers, siblings, cousins, neighbors, all the left behind, and even the strangers who ambled through cemeteries to "Oooh" and "Aaah" at the beauty of the stones, the wonder of the ancient dates, the odd names, the imagined lives? In many ways, Digger could feel bad for Danny's mother, but she did get one continual connection from his choice to de-connect: For the rest of her long life, whenever Mrs. Jones looked at the sea, at its glittering surface, its awesome circumference, its ageless scent and timeless stirring, she could think of her boy, who had become a part of it all now, who had finally found a place where he belonged.

Shortly after the swastika tribunal, the administrators called for another meeting involving another Nazi, one who conquered grammatical errors with a twitch of her red pen. It was to be the launching of the U.S.S. Grammar Nazi into retirement. Nobody cracked champagne over Professor Schmidt's head, but plenty of the bubbly disappeared into it. The ceremony took place in the Admin Building's lounge, equipped with a bar, false fireplace, and lush vinyl chairs, all usually reserved for gatherings of charitable alumnae or future ones' progenitors.

Looking flushed and too young to retire, the Humanities Chair gave a short speech in which she handed her leadership position over to Bob Redlen (Tobias Mann grimacing visibly), who himself was set to retire in five years. Then Gwena surprised everyone by referencing her nickname to end her formal farewell: "OVC has had its share of Nazis this past year, but they are all gone now. Nazi free! [Everyone cheered, warmed by the champagne but doused a bit by the Nazi reference, which was better left under a rock.] Most of you no doubt know that some students labeled me the Grammar Nazi. [She looked about at smiling, nodding faces.] Now I will be gone, too, but I hope and know that my colleagues will continue to expect only the best from our students so that their writing will reflect only the best about this fine institution."

As the ending of a career, these words were a bit odd and abrupt, even when she finished them with "Thank you." For a frightening moment, Digger thought that she was going to throw her right arm out and cry "Heil," but he recovered and began to clap, the rest of the crowd following the sound after realizing that the short speech was over. All of the full-time Humanities faculty attended, and to the Chair's credit, close to a dozen adjuncts took the time to wish their leader a bon voyage (and perhaps to get some champagne, too). Amid the applause, the Grammar Nazi disappeared into the crowd, and after the celebration, Gwena Schmidt vanished from most of their lives. Her last spoken words to Digger? "Watch out for the worms," of course.

In the parking lot after Schmidt's farewell party, Digger spotted Richard, the maintenance man, just arriving for work. He greeted the elder fellow warmly, partly due to the champagne bubbling through his body.

"Professor Diggerson," said Richard, "I want to say good-bye to you, for this is my last day. I'm retiring."

So many good-byes, thought Digger sadly, but instead he declared, "Congratulations, Richard. You don't look old enough to retire. Do you have any plans?"

"I am going to relax," said the elderly man, smiling.

"That's a good plan," said Digger, adding, "We will miss you." Then, because he wasn't sure what else to say, Digger asked, "Who's going to replace you, I mean, do your job?"

Richard laughed. "Do you know Dan Pinsky?"

Digger said that he did not.

"You will," said Richard, and the old man laughed again.

Smiling, the maintenance man then turned and walked off into the campus, and frowning, the professor ambled off.

This little connection marked the end of the spring semester, for Digger would not have to step on the OVC campus again until the annual summer meetings, the first in July for the full-time composition professors, the second in August including all the part-timers, a handful of new ones each year, along with a few missing faces from past semesters (more good-byes). At home that May and all through June, Digger expected

Anna to return "that day," listened for her tires grinding into the driveway, paused to separate and classify any foreign sounds from the bay's continuous breathing. Dozens of times throughout the day, he looked out back, scanning horizons both far and near.

Shyla did not return. Every dusk, the most poignant time of the Earth's spinning voyage, a moment for memories and ghosts and possibilities, Digger would sit on his back steps and wait for her, sometimes for both her and Skittles, and sometimes for both cats and Anna. Sometimes he would drink one can, two cans, even three Buds as he watched the night swallow the world. After nights like those, Digger would awaken grateful that he did not carry any addiction genes within his blood, for he knew that if he had, then life would spiral into something even worse. If he *had* a life, he would think.

All through the early summer, though, he anticipated his wife's return. He even prepared for it. To make the cottage more homey, Digger bought a blue spruce accent tree, not a bushy blue monster that would one day tower above and dwarf the cottage, but the spindly kind, less branches, a thinner trunk, more like the essence of a thicker blue spruce, and in the wind this spirit tree would sway in all directions at once, its furry shorter upper part waving frenetically, two longer bottom branches swinging in opposing symmetry like an umpire calling a runner safe at home. Feeling the spruce's pulsing life, Digger thought of Anna's broken boy, Tommy, who would no doubt have clamped his thin arms around this tree and never let go. *Never let go.* To accent the little tree, to trim it, Digger brought the birds by attaching a tube feeder to a pole near the blue spruce, and soon the backdrop of pushing-pulling sea sounds carried the verse of "Chicka-dee-dee-dee," along with a varied chorus of chirps, some sounding like happy statements, others like thoughtful questions. Blue Jays would land in trios on different spruce branches and peruse the grounds before screeching and then blashing into the tube feeder for a seed, one at a time. Sparrows would land in a manageable flock on the ground itself, one small brown body and then another, choreographed, like little Spitfires in the World War II runway of a seaside English village. At dusk, the cardinals would cast their single cheeps to the twilight, calling to the stars to light their lamps. Creating this beautiful outer world, Digger fed his inner one, too.

Throughout the long days, birds came—individually, in families, and in flocks—but no little cats, and no Anna. Still, Digger maintained his deep sense of loyalty, a wall that kept his dark river from overflowing, roots that bound ethics to both reality and fantasy, both symbolized by the back of a tombstone that read, "Listen, you can hear them sing." Their union had turned existence into song. It had existed, so it did exist. He and Anna were beauty, light, energy, timeless. Not until August did Digger truly recognize that Anna's *phase* was something bigger, not just a "choice" with a lowercase "c"—a simple step reversible by her return that night, the next morning, *soon*—but a leap from one world into another, one with no return ticket. Not so different than the step Danny Jones had taken to fly briefly, but in Anna's case nobody had actually died, just a marriage.

A couple weeks before the fall semester's commencement, Digger found a big brown packet in the mail, "Return Requested" stamped above his address, the return being a lawyer's office. "Junk mail!" Digger said to himself, opening the package (*heavy in hand or just mind?*) with some trepidation, thinking of a vampire hunter's easing up a casket lid. And it was a casket, of course: divorce papers.

In the summary of why Anna was requesting a divorce, she had said (or the lawyer had paraphrased) a fragment that Digger wrote into a notebook and studied every day for weeks, every week for months, and every month for years: "Irreconcilable differences involving present and future." The two lawyerly words, "Irreconcilable differences," broached no counter argument, no room for debate, for opinion formed their crusty armor, but what of the vague reference to past and future. What differences were those? Digger asked himself that question a thousand times, a million, pounding it into his consciousness and drowning it in his dreams, but no answers came. Anna had wanted no children, so he had agreed. Did she now want them? What differences could be so sudden and so "irreconcilable"? She had told him that she wanted to be free. *Free,* a word with claws. Free of what, of him? *Of him!* Or maybe of her mother. Maybe Anna had become her lost father.

After a week of turmoil, of arguments that rose heroically in his mind and then fell, cut to pieces, Digger signed where requested and returned the documents, driving to the post office to deliver the brown envelope to the anonymity of the drive-by box, rather than placing it in his own mailbox and thinking of it out there, ticking like a bomb. After this act, he did not feel lighter, did not himself feel *free.* And the next day his mother called in agony (so that Digger at first thought, "How did she find out!"), in bursts of tears (the only time he had ever heard her cry, including after news of his father's death), saying over and over that "Emma was gone," that "Emma was dead," that his sister "crashed her car" just like their father, that she herself "could not stand it, simply could not," that "a parent should not outlive a child."

Jean Diggerson's final words were probably responsible for keeping her remaining child from following a path laid out by a sad black boy into the sky.

Epilogue

Fast forward now, a couple of years. Digger himself would admit that in that time his life was not worth viewing, for who would want to watch a man sitting alone in his living room, listening to the stillness ("Was that the back door?"), staring at the silence ("No"), waiting, waiting? He worked, he came home, he watched TV, he took walks on the beach, looking in every back yard for black-and-white cats. He learned that walking alone and eating alone were similar, both creating lumps below the heart. He read, devoured Mankell, revisited Hillerman, tried other mystery writers but often found their protagonists too perfect, always understanding situations, making just the right moves, saying witty things, and getting the girl, always getting the girl.

Digger worked, he gazed at the sea, at the rush of gulls and clouds, he drank, he often got stinking drunk, he shrank, he raged, he drove his truck into a tree, he got arrested, he took responsibility, he survived, he got a new truck, he paid more for insurance, he paid, he woke up a bit, and he died a bit more. On the phone, he talked to his mother, he thought of Emma, he missed her, missed his father, missed Skittles and especially Shyla, missed his old life, his old dead life. He lived in a prison with Anna's ghost. With old photos, old letters from Anna, objects of hers left in the house (a hair brush, a coffee cup, a book), and often with alcohol, Digger tried hard to stop time and to rewind it, to discover where things went wrong, to fix those tangles, which his mind fingers could never really grasp. The knots were too tight and complex.

He thought of Danny Jones less and less, the image of the boy with giant white eyes perched within the heavens over the yawning mouth of Hell fading, retreating into shadow. Often now, Digger became Danny, hovering in the windy night above the pitiless pit. Of course, Digger occasionally contemplated following Danny down, taking that path to the Bay Bridge, that sweet exit, that siren's song, but he never really came close to the drive. How could he do that to his mother? *Perhaps when she was gone.*

But stories require happy endings, do they not? Each night, no matter how long, dark, and silent, ends in a dawn, in a new beginning, in the warm smell of coffee, sometimes even in a loving "Good morning" or at least the golden kisses of a cat's eyes. Okay, then, here is an end to the tale of Digger and Anna, of Danny and the Bridge, the best kind of conclusion because it leads to another beginning.

Two years AA (After Anna), Professor Matthew Diggerson, his temples throbbing after a night of yeastly company and solace, drove toward the docks, passing many weekend empty buildings, some obviously vacant during the week (many broken windows, some patched and boarded), and searched for one that the website's directions said was down this Service Center road. The summer sun annoyed his head, and the sea gulls clustering and gliding, *like vultures*, in the hazy, bright sky told the driver that sea water was within a stone's throw, meaning that he was coming to the place or had missed it. *There it was!*

When he pulled open the door to the non-descript cinder-block building, surrounded by ugly chain-link fencing, Digger encountered a cacophony of frenzied barking, a wave of chaos that almost drove him from the animal shelter back into the harsh light of day.

"You get used to it," a female animal-control officer said from the window of a walled-off office.

"Can I look at the dogs?" said Digger.

"If you have ear plugs," said the woman, motioning him with her left arm and head to the door on his right. When Digger opened that one, the volume of canine adrenaline rose even higher, creating magnified doubt, but he stepped into the darkened kennel area anyway. He walked fairly quickly past all the cages, most of the dogs pushing right into their bars to reach him, to connect, barking happily (it now seemed to him), tongues extended impossibly, tails a battering blur, and Digger realized that the noise no doubt erupted whenever anyone pulled into the pound's driveway. *It was the call of hope.* The chaos of sound held mostly joy, optimism, just a few shadows of fear and uncertainty, which Digger could see in some of the cells, where the dogs held themselves back and barked questions, not greetings, at the intruder and at their own dark instinct. Twice, the man strolled the rectangular inner pathway by the pens, the cages, a couple dozen at least, and after his second circuit, Digger stood before the very first kennel on the right, gazing at a dog who had not greeted him, who had made no noises at all, a medium-sized animal, skinny and tan with a blackened muzzle, *and what was that?* Some extra hair ruffled behind its broad head. *An odd looking dog.* Lying head to tail in a little puddle of emotion—sadness, acceptance, fear? Then, when the creature's brown eyes moved up to his face, Digger understood all. He fell in love.

"Hello," he said. "You look like a little lion."

The little lion dog's mouth broke open, a sigh escaping, a silly grin forming. Digger grinned back.

"I think I'll call you Simba."

THE END

ABOUT THE AUTHOR

 After graduating from the University of Connecticut and then Arizona, Dave returned to New England to teach college composition and continues to do so. In Providence, Rhode Island, he lives happily with his wife (Elena) and two dogs (Belle and Holly). His "Simba" passed away peacefully in 2013 at the age of 16.

www.ingramcontent.com/pod-product-compliance
Lightning Source LLC
Chambersburg PA
CBHW020314260626
47156CB00004B/1225